D1432327

The only people with whom you should try to get even are those who have been kind to you.

—An Amish Proverb

SUGARCREEK AMISH MYSTERIES

Blessings in Disguise
Where Hope Dwells
The Buggy before the Horse
A Season of Secrets
O Little Town of Sugarcreek
Off the Beaten Path
Peace Like a River
Simply Vanished
A Stitch in Time
Mason Jar Mayhem
When There's a Will
Shoo, Fly, Shoo!
Earthly Treasures
No Time for Trouble
All Abuzz at the Honey Bee
Home Sweet Sugarcreek
Blessed Are the Cheese Makers
Stranger Things Have Happened
In a Jam

In a Jam

SUGARCREEK Amish MYSTERIES

ELIZABETH ADAMS

Guideposts

New York

Sugarcreek Amish Mysteries is a trademark of Guideposts.

Published by Guideposts Books & Inspirational Media
110 William Street
New York, NY 10038
Guideposts.org

Cover and interior design by Müllerhaus
Cover illustration by Bill Bruning, represented by Deborah Wolfe, LTD.
Typeset by Aptara, Inc.

Printed and bound in the United States of America
10 9 8 7 6 5 4 3 2 1

CHAPTER ONE

Cheryl Cooper had just finished ringing up the last of the customers from a tour group, and she took a deep breath and let it out slowly. She was used to large groups descending upon the Swiss Miss, the gift shop she ran in the heart of Ohio's Amish country, but usually February was a quiet time of year. So far this month, however, she'd seen brisker sales than she expected. *Hey, I'm not complaining,* she thought as she leaned against the counter to rest for a moment. But she did enjoy the way things usually slowed down a bit this time of year.

"I thought they were going to buy every last piece of cheese," Esther Miller said, gesturing toward the cooler of locally handcrafted hard cheeses along the side wall. She edged around the counter and reached underneath to pull out a rag. "We will need to order more soon."

"I'll do that today," Cheryl said. She purchased as much of her merchandise as possible from nearby Amish families, and she had recently started stocking a smoked cheddar that had been flying off the shelves. "Have you noticed anything else we're running low on?"

Esther stopped, thought for a moment, and then said, "I think we will need more soap soon as well. That new honeysuckle scent is really selling well."

"There's more in the storage room. I'll put out what we have and get some more in." Cheryl nodded and made a quick note to get more. Then she took a deep breath, pushed herself up, and looked around the shop. Esther had moved around the counter and was running the dust cloth along the shelf of hand-carved wooden toys, her cheerful red apron swaying over her long Amish dress as she moved. Despite the large group that had come through, the shelves were relatively neat. There were two women browsing the selection of handmade pot holders, and Ben and Rueben Vogel played checkers at the small table by the front window. Otherwise the store was quiet. The potbellied stove in the corner kept the store toasty warm despite blustery wind that tossed delicate flakes of snow outside the heart-shaped window.

Just as she turned to go to the storage room, the front door of the shop opened and a man stepped inside, bundled up in a long wool coat and a thick maroon scarf. He kicked the door shut, looked around, and, seeing Cheryl, stormed straight to the back of the shop. Cheryl stopped and watched as he approached. He was heavyset, with pink cheeks and wisps of gray hair that spilled out from under his hat. She watched him carefully. He looked the teensiest bit familiar, though she couldn't say where she knew him from.

"Are you the owner of this place?" he asked—*demanded* might be a better word—as he set a paper bag down on the wooden counter. He pulled off his leather gloves and adjusted his wire-rimmed glasses, which had steamed up when he entered the shop. He looked to be in his early sixties, though it was hard to say exactly.

"I run the store," Cheryl said, nodding. Technically the store was owned by her aunt Mitzi, who had left Cheryl in charge when she went to Papua New Guinea to serve as a missionary. But Cheryl was in charge of things these days. "What can I help you with?"

"My wife bought this here on Saturday." He reached into the paper bag and pulled out what Cheryl immediately recognized to be a jar of Naomi Miller's homemade strawberry jam. It was one of the store's best-selling items, with good reason. Naomi used fruit she'd grown in her own garden, and her recipe highlighted the sweetness and freshness of the fruit. It was delicious. But why was this man bringing the jar back?

"Is there a problem with the jam?" Cheryl asked as politely as she could. She'd never heard any complaints about the jam before. Out of the corner of her eye she could see that Esther was watching the exchange carefully, waiting to see what the man would say about her mother's jam.

"Yeah, I'd say there's a problem with the jam," the man said. "My wife had some of it on a shortbread cookie before bed last night, and she got sick from it. She was up half the night running to the bathroom, and her stomach hurts so badly she couldn't even get out of bed this morning. It's the last day of our vacation and she's spending it lying around the hotel room, puking." He unscrewed the lid of the jar and held it out. Cheryl looked at the jam. It looked normal to her.

"Oh dear. I am so sorry to hear she's not feeling well," Cheryl said carefully. She felt badly for the man and his wife. It was awful to be sick when you were away from home, and to have it ruin a day of their vacation was no doubt incredibly frustrating. But Cheryl was struggling to understand how he was so certain the jam was to blame.

"Had she been feeling ill before?" She reached out to take the jam, and he let it go reluctantly. Cheryl looked down at it. It was just like every other jar of jam Naomi produced. The jellied fruit was packed into a small mason jar with a raised diamond pattern, and the lid was brass. The label was written in Naomi's own looping handwriting. Cheryl sniffed the jam. She didn't know what jam would smell like if it had gone bad, but this smelled normal. Like summer and sunshine and all the things this dreary February day was not.

"No." The man looked at her like she was an idiot. "Like I said, she didn't get sick until after she ate this 'wholesome homemade jam.'" He made air quotes with his fingers, echoing the words Cheryl had used to describe the jam on the sign tacked to the shelf.

Cheryl saw that the women who had been looking at the pot holders were now headed out the door, and Ben and Rueben had been disturbed from their game and now were watching this confrontation unfold.

"I am so sorry to hear this," Cheryl said. "Of course we will refund the price of the jam." That seemed to mollify him a bit.

"But are you certain it was the jam that made her ill?" Cheryl asked this as gently as she could. "We've never had any problems with the jam before. The Amish woman who makes it is a very good friend of mine, and I know she's very conscientious. Could it have been something else she ate that upset her stomach?"

"First of all, she doesn't have an 'upset stomach.'" The man made air quotes again. "She's vomiting up blood. And I'm certain it was the jam." The man's face was getting redder. "She started to feel ill shortly after she ate it. And the cookies she ate it with were the same ones she eats every night before bed. We brought them from home, and she had some the previous night with no problems. It was only after she had the jam that she began to get sick."

Cheryl felt badly for the woman and hoped she would heal quickly. But she was dubious that the jam was at fault. Cheryl trusted Naomi over this guy any day. And it was flu season. It was much more likely his wife had picked up a virus somewhere than Naomi's jam had somehow made her sick.

She knew that the right thing to do was to give this man his money back. She'd had customers ask for returns from time to time, and she was generally happy to oblige. But something about the way this man was staring at her, like she was somehow personally responsible for his wife's illness, was grating.

"Of course," she said and opened the register. She counted the bills and held them out for the man. He took the bills in one hand, and with the other he pulled a smooth leather wallet from his pocket. He deposited the bills inside and stuffed it back into his pocket.

Cheryl expected him to turn and go, but he stood there like he was expecting her to say something more.

"Is there anything else?" she said as politely as she could. This man's superior air was grating, and she was finding it increasingly difficult to remain cheerful.

"Well?" he said, widening his eyes. "I just told you the jam made my wife violently ill. Aren't you going to take the rest of the jam off the shelves so that no one else gets sick from this stuff?" He gestured toward the shelf of jam along the main aisle of the store. Cheryl noticed that his gold wedding ring cut into his finger.

Oh. Goodness. He wanted her to clear out all of her inventory. She didn't say anything for a moment, struggling to find the right words to use to respond to him.

"I'll certainly look into it," she said, forcing a smile on to her face.

He stared at her, his mouth open. "I just told you that this jam made my wife violently ill, and you're going to continue to sell it?" His voice boomed. "My wife is vomiting up blood, and it's because of this jam that she bought here. What kind of irresponsible businessperson would continue to sell this stuff?"

Cheryl forced herself to bite back all of the answers that came to mind. Her father had always said that her temper matched her red hair, and she could feel it flaring up now. But she knew that she needed to maintain a polite demeanor, no matter what this man said to her. She would count to ten before she answered, she decided, so she would have time to...

"Excuse me?" It took a moment for the voice to register in Cheryl's racing mind. But then she looked over and saw Ben Vogel standing next to the man. She hadn't even noticed him approaching. "I'm sorry to interrupt, but I couldn't help overhearing."

People two counties over couldn't help overhearing, Cheryl thought, and then started over counting at one again.

"Did you say your wife is vomiting blood?" Ben asked. Ben's soft-spoken nature betrayed his Amish upbringing, but his jeans and running shoes marked him as English. He had been distanced from his family—including his brother Rueben—for many decades after he left the church, and the two brothers had started meeting here to play checkers just about every day some time ago.

The man nodded. "More than once. And this lousy excuse for a..."

"I'm a doctor," Ben said, interrupting the man. "If she's vomiting blood, that's serious. Does she have other symptoms?"

The man seemed confused for a minute. He looked from Ben's frail frame over to Rueben, in his Amish clothes and long gray beard, and back to Ben.

"I'm retired now," Ben said in answer to the unspoken question. "I was raised Amish, but I left the church to go to medical school. I treated patients for decades. And I am worried about what you've said so far. Does she have other symptoms?"

"Nausea," he said slowly. "Vomiting, like I said."

"Anything else?"

He thought for a moment. "Her nose started bleeding this morning, but that could have been..."

"A nosebleed?"

The man nodded warily. Cheryl was surprised. It wasn't like Ben to interrupt.

"Where is your wife now?" Ben said.

"We're staying over at the Village Inn Bed-and-Breakfast. She's in the room."

Ben shook his head. "You need to take her to the emergency room to get checked out right away. It may be nothing, but her symptoms are serious enough that she needs medical attention."

"Are you for real?" The man was watching Ben, evaluating.

"Yes," Ben said. "Please, even if it turns out to be nothing, it's still a good idea to have her seen."

"All right," the man said, warming to the idea. "Okay, I will take her." He started to turn toward the door, but then he turned back toward Cheryl. "If there's something seriously wrong with her, you'll be hearing from my lawyers."

And with that, he turned, shoved his hands into his coat pockets, and stormed out the door.

"He was not a happy customer," Esther said.

Cheryl had to laugh at her typically Amish way of understating the situation.

"Were you serious about his wife needing to go to the emergency room?" Cheryl asked.

"Very." Ben nodded. "Again, it may be nothing. And even if it is something, I'm sure it has nothing to do with the jam."

Rueben was still sitting at the table by the window, but he was listening intently. Esther was also listening, though she continued to dust the shelves.

"But what do you think it is?" Cheryl asked.

"It's hard to say." Ben looked down at the counter. "But those symptoms are serious, no matter what caused them."

Cheryl studied him. She trusted Ben's opinion. He had left the Amish to study medicine after his mother had died of an illness that antibiotics could have treated. He was a good, honest man, and though he was no longer Amish, his faith spoke through everything he did. Now he was shifting from one foot to the other, looking down. There was something he wasn't saying.

"But you have a guess what might have caused the symptoms, don't you?" Cheryl asked.

Ben shrugged but then let out a breath. "It is dangerous to try to diagnose a patient based on a secondhand account of symptoms." He paused for a moment and seemed to think through what he was going to say next. "But I will say this: I once had a patient, a little girl, come into my office. She was nauseous, vomiting blood. She'd had strange bruising, and her nose had started bleeding as well. It turned out she'd accidentally ingested rat poison."

"Rat poison?" Cheryl was confused. Did people even use rat poison these days? And what could that possibly have to do with this man's wife?

Ben nodded. "I got them to take her to the hospital right away, and they pumped her stomach and gave her medication to counteract the poison. They were able to save her life but just barely." He shook his head. "If they had waited much longer to get her treated, I'm not sure she would have survived."

"You don't really think this man's wife ate rat poison though. Do you?" Cheryl said, shaking her head.

"Like I said, I don't know what this woman's problem is. And I agree with you that it probably has nothing to do with the jam. But I do know that it's better to be safe than sorry."

"Of course it is," Cheryl said. "And it sounds like no matter what caused the problem, she needs our prayers."

Ben nodded. "You are absolutely right." He eyed the jar, which was sitting on the counter.

"What is it?" she asked, gesturing at the jar. "Do you see anything odd?"

Ben shook his head. "I was just wondering if... Well, again, it very likely is not the jam that made the woman sick. But I was wondering if we should have it tested, just to be sure."

"Tested?"

"A friend of mine runs a toxicology lab nearby. I could ask him to take a look. Just to eliminate the possibility that something was added to the jam, of course," he said.

Cheryl thought about this for a moment. It seemed a bit much, if there really was no way the jam had made the woman sick. But then, if Ben's friend tested it, they could say for sure that the jam was not responsible. It would be nice to have that assurance, not just for her own peace of mind, but also in case the man turned out to be litigious. She hated to even think like that, but the reality of running a business today was that she needed to worry about things like lawsuits from angry tourists who believed they had been poisoned. If Ben had the jam tested, at least they could have evidence on their side if worse came to worst.

"That's a good idea." Cheryl screwed the lid back on the jam and slid it across the counter toward him. "Why don't you take it?" She reached under the counter and pulled out a bag and handed it to Ben, and he nodded and put the jar inside the bag. He promised to take it to his friend's lab as soon as he finished his checkers game. Then he went back over to the table where his brother was waiting.

Cheryl tried not to worry. The woman would be fine. And Cheryl would pray for her, whoever she was. She hoped that she would be well and she would recover from whatever it was that had laid her low. Still, as Ben went back to finish up his game and Esther moved on to dust another part of the store, Cheryl couldn't help wondering: Was there any chance it *was* the jam that had made her sick?

Chapter Two

Cheryl tried not to let the encounter with the man get to her. As Ben had said, even if his wife had ingested poison somehow, there was no way it could have come from Naomi's jam.

Besides, *poison*? It was like something out of a Victorian novel. But still, she couldn't stop thinking about it, even after Levi picked up Esther and Cheryl started to close up the shop for the night. She was just finishing closing out the register when the phone rang.

"Hello. Thank you for calling the Swiss Miss."

"Is this Cheryl?"

"Yes," Cheryl said hesitantly.

"Oh, Cheryl, this is Heather. Over at the Honey Bee? I'm so sorry to ask this, but I was wondering if there's any way you could do me a favor. Well, do Kathy a favor, really."

"Of course." Kathy Kimble was Cheryl's good friend, and Cheryl was happy to help her.

"Kathy got really sick today, so Keith took her to the doctor, and I'm left here alone." Cheryl knew Keith was Kathy's new husband. He was a sweet man, and Cheryl was very happy for Kathy. "I started to clean up for the night, but I have to leave in about two minutes go pick up my mom, who is getting chemo treatments over in New Philadelphia. If I don't get her, she'll be sitting there alone waiting for me, and I just don't want to make her do that right now. Again, I'm so sorry to ask this, but I know you've helped Kathy open and close up here in the past, and I was wondering if there is any way you could..." She let her voice drift off, obviously hesitant to even ask.

"Of course, I'll be happy to help. I'll be right over," Cheryl said immediately. Certainly she'd help out her friend. But she wanted to go back to something else Heather had said. "But what's wrong with Kathy? I hope she's okay?"

"I hope she is too," Heather said. "She was fine earlier, and then after lunch she started to feel nauseous. Then she started—well, she was running to the bathroom a lot. At first she was joking that she hoped she wasn't pregnant, but then I think it got worse and she was pretty sure that wasn't what was wrong. I think she said something about blood. That's when she called Keith to come get her and take her to the hospital."

"Oh dear. I sure hope she's all right." That sounded terrible. And, actually, it sounded very much like the symptoms the angry man had described of his wife. Cheryl hesitated, and then she decided to ask the question that occurred to her. "She didn't eat any of Naomi Miller's jam, did she?" She'd meant it somewhat as a joke, but as the words came out, she realized it didn't sound like it.

"Actually, she did," Heather said. "I saw her open a jar and use some on her turkey sandwich at lunch. I teased her about it because I don't see how turkey and strawberry jam go together, but she said it's just like using cranberry sauce at Thanksgiving, and she slathered it right on."

"Oh." Cheryl felt like she should say something more, but that was all she could get out.

"I'm sorry, Cheryl, but I really have to run. Do you think you could..."

"Of course. I'll be right over."

Cheryl ended the call. Was there any chance...

But that was crazy. There was no way Naomi's jam had made Kathy sick. It had to have been something else. Maybe she really was pregnant. Or maybe the turkey on her sandwich was bad. It couldn't have been the jam. She hoped Ben's test results came back soon. She locked up her shop and hurried across the street to the Honey Bee.

A very relieved Heather handed her the spare key and ran off, and Cheryl went through the familiar routine of closing up the café.

She found a newly opened jar of Naomi's strawberry jam in the refrigerator, and she sniffed it, but it smelled perfectly normal. She thought about spreading some on a piece of a leftover muffin to taste it but hesitated. Was there any chance something was off with it? As she moved the leftover sandwiches to the industrial refrigerator, she wondered whether it was possible a batch of the jam had gone bad. Cheryl had heard of food poisoning that could happen if bacteria found its way into canned food. Botulism, she thought it was called. But wasn't the food supposed to smell rancid in that case? This just smelled like everyday jam.

Cheryl didn't know. Still, as she hauled out the trash and wiped down the counters, she couldn't stop thinking about the possibility it could be true.

After Cheryl had locked up the Honey Bee and left the spare key under the doormat, as Heather had instructed, she made her way back to her parking space behind the Swiss Miss and climbed into her car. Night fell early these days, and it was dark and cold. Her headlights illuminated flakes of softly falling snow. Cheryl had been planning to head home, but as she climbed into her car, she thought she might instead pop over to visit her close friend Naomi Miller.

Not to ask if her jam was tainted, of course. But to give her a heads-up about the events of the day. It was only fair to let her know what that man was saying about her jam, after all, Cheryl reasoned.

Of course, it didn't hurt that the Miller house, full of life and family and laughter, sounded much more appealing than her own lonely house on this winter evening. And hey, the fact that she might get to see Levi was an added bonus. Not that that was why she was going.

Cheryl pulled on to Route 39 and headed out of town. The buildings of downtown slowly gave way to open space. The snow was falling a bit thicker now, slanting down at her windshield, lit up by the headlights. Cheryl was used to driving in weather like this, and she had good snow tires on her car. She wasn't worried about the roads, though she knew it might be difficult for buggies to traverse the roads on a night like tonight. Cheryl genuinely liked snow, and it was always so exciting the first few times it fell in winter. But by mid-February, even she was ready to be done with it and was already longing for signs of spring. But it would still be several weeks before the daffodils started to push their way up through the dirt, and as the snow fell thick through the dark night, spring felt very far away.

In the past, Cheryl had gone skiing at this time of year. Her father had loved the sport, and when she and her brother were children, he had saved up and taken them skiing at least once every winter. He had patiently taught both of his children how to control their speed and how to turn and how to love the feeling of wind against their faces as they zoomed down the mountain. As they got older, Cheryl's brother, Matt, had taken up snowboarding, but Cheryl had always preferred the way skiing allowed you to be more in control. Those had been special times, those long days on the mountain with her family.

Then, in more recent years, she had often gone skiing with her ex-fiancé Lance. Lance had grown up skiing competitively, and he had loved to spend winter days sailing down the mountain at breakneck speed. Cheryl hadn't loved the adrenaline rush of doing black diamonds at as fast a pace as possible like he did, but she had to agree that for some reason, zooming down mountain slopes made the snow seem less like a punishment to be endured and more like a treat. The way the wind shrieked as it blew past your ears; the way the mountain just opened up in ways you could never imagine from the ground; the quiet and peacefulness of the world from the ski lift—it was like nothing else. It made winter fun.

But that all seemed like a different lifetime. She didn't even know if there was somewhere to ski around here. In the year she'd lived in Sugarcreek, she'd never heard of one. Maybe that was something she could look into. It might be fun to gather some friends and give it a shot. At least it would be better than cursing the snow and waiting for the bitterly cold months to pass.

A few minutes later, she pulled up in front of the Miller house. The driveway had been recently plowed, and she had no trouble pulling up in front of the house. Cheryl had laughed out loud the first time she'd seen a V-shaped horse-drawn snowplow, but the Amish way of clearing snow really worked. Most Amish families around here cleared their driveways this way.

Cheryl turned off her engine. She could see dim lights in the barn. The men were still doing the evening chores then. Ugh. She couldn't imagine mucking out stalls when the weather was in single digits like this. She climbed out of the car and made her way up the porch steps. She stomped her feet on the welcome mat, and a moment later, Elizabeth Miller, Naomi's older daughter, welcomed her into the house.

On some level, Cheryl knew that the Miller home, lit by kerosene lamps and heated by the stove and fireplace, was actually darker and cooler than most English homes, but it always felt bright and warm to Cheryl as she stepped inside and was greeted by her friend and her daughters.

"It is good to see you. And how wonderful that you made it out here on a night like tonight," Naomi said. "I hope you did not have any trouble driving here?" She took Cheryl's coat and hung it by the front door. "Please come in and warm up. We are just cleaning up. Would you like some soup? It is potato leek, and I made far too much."

Cheryl hesitated. In college, she'd had a guy friend who was notorious for showing up whenever Cheryl and her roommates were about to eat, and they joked about how he only liked them for their food. Cheryl didn't want to appear to be like Dave, always showing up just in time for food. But then, there was *always* delicious food around this house. And she knew that Naomi didn't believe she came just for the food. Sharing her food was how Naomi showed her love. Besides, Cheryl was hungry, and it did smell wonderful...

"Elizabeth, please get her a bowl," Naomi said, smiling. The girl complied quickly, and moments later a steaming bowl of soup and a hunk of homemade bread were placed in front of her. Elizabeth's dark hair was tucked up under her *kapp*, and the girl was quiet and studious. Sometimes she was so quiet you could forget she was in the room.

"So," Naomi said, sliding into a chair next to Cheryl, "Esther told me about the man who says my jam made his wife ill. Do you know if his wife is doing any better? I have been worried about her."

"I don't know," Cheryl said. That was so like Naomi—accused of poisoning somebody, she worried about the sick woman. "But something strange happened later, after Esther left for the day."

"Yes?" Naomi said. Elizabeth placed a steaming mug of tea in front of each of them.

"Thank you," Cheryl said, and Elizabeth smiled and looked away quickly.

"*Danki,*" Naomi said. Elizabeth nodded, and then she took a cup for herself and moved off into the living room. From here, Cheryl could see that Esther was already there, sewing.

"So after Esther left today, I got a call from Heather at the Honey Bee. She asked me to help clean up tonight because Kathy Kimble was ill."

"Oh dear. I hope something is not going around. My Seth has been feeling a bit under the weather as well. Or..." Naomi's eyes widened. "Do you think a little one is on the way?"

"No, I don't think that's it," Cheryl said. Naomi looked disappointed. "Actually, from what Heather said, she seemed to have the same sort of symptoms as the other woman." Cheryl spooned some of the soup and blew on it. Tiny curls of steam wafted up.

"That is terrible." Naomi shook her head.

"The thing is, Heather says that Kathy also had some of the strawberry jam."

"What?" Naomi shook her head. "Oh, Cheryl, you do not think..."

"I don't know," Cheryl said and ate the bite of soup to give herself a few moments to think. "Of course I don't think you did anything wrong," she said carefully. "More than likely, it's just a weird coincidence, and it has nothing to do with your jam at all." She thought back to what Ben had said about rat poison and about its symptoms. Was there any chance…? "But I was wondering if there was any possibility that the jars could have gone bad somehow?"

"Oh, Cheryl, I certainly hope not," Naomi said. Her hands were wrapped so tightly around her mug that her knuckles had gone white, and her face was pale. "I do not know. I suppose it is possible. But I am careful. I have been making jam all my life, and it has never happened." It sounded like she was trying to convince herself as much as Cheryl.

"How does it work?" Cheryl asked gently. "Can you tell me what the process is for making jam?"

Naomi's face relaxed, and she gave a tiny laugh. "Have you never made jam?"

"No, I haven't." Cheryl smiled. She knew making jam, like baking bread and any number of other wholesome activities, was an everyday routine for the Amish. But before she'd moved to Amish country, she'd thought jam came from the condiments aisle at the supermarket. She didn't even know how you would start.

"You must come over next time we do a batch. You will enjoy it."

Cheryl nodded. She wasn't so sure about that. She'd read *Little Women* and remembered Meg's breakdown when she couldn't get her currant jelly to gel. It seemed a lot harder than Naomi was making it out to be. She spooned another mouthful of the hot soup and gestured for Naomi to go on.

"The process is really quite simple," Naomi said. "I use mostly fruit we've grown here, though sometimes I buy some at a farm stand.

But you wash and cut up the berries, and then you boil them, along with the sugar and pectin, until they reach the right consistency."

"What is pectin?"

"Ah. It is a substance that allows the fruit to gel. Some people use grated orange or lemon peels, since it is found in the skins of those fruits, but I think it works better to use store-bought powdered pectin."

Cheryl nodded. That made sense. And so far the process didn't seem all that hard.

"How do you know when it's the right consistency?"

Naomi looked flummoxed. "I do not know. You just do."

Okay, maybe it was a bit harder than she'd first thought.

"And then what?" Cheryl asked.

"And then you pour the jam into your jars. The only difficult thing is that you must be very careful to only use jars that are perfectly clean, so you must use sterilized jars."

"How do you sterilize the jars?" Cheryl broke off a hunk of bread.

"We use a very large pot and boil them. This kills off any bacteria, so the jam will not spoil. Then we pour the hot jam into the jars and put on the lids, and then we boil the full jars. Then we take them out and let them cool, and they seal as the temperature drops. And then they're ready."

Cheryl thought this through. She knew the satisfying sound a jar of jam made when you opened it for the first time. She knew that was the seal being broken. "How do you know when the jars are sealed?"

"When the jars are cooling, they make a popping sound as the jam inside cools."

Cheryl thought about it and realized that a vacuum must be created inside the jar by the cooling, contracting air. That must be what made the seal airtight.

"Is there any chance that a few of the jars might not have sealed properly?" Cheryl asked. She felt awful even asking, knowing it must feel like she was accusing Naomi. But Naomi seemed unaffected.

"I suppose it is possible," Naomi said. "Though I test each jar before I put it away and again before I put on a label and sell it to you." She thought for a moment and then called out to Elizabeth in the other room.

The girl appeared in the kitchen moments later, and then Naomi said something in Pennsylvania Dutch that Cheryl couldn't understand. Elizabeth nodded, and then she disappeared down the steps that led to the basement. Cheryl ate a few bites of her soup, and moments later Elizabeth returned carrying a jar of Naomi's blueberry jam.

"Danki," Naomi said, and Elizabeth nodded and went back into the living room.

"This jar is sealed," Naomi said, holding it out. "See, when you push on the dimple in the lid, it should not spring up." She demonstrated. "If it does spring up, or if the jar does not make this sound"—she tapped on the lid with a spoon she'd grabbed from the counter, and a clear, ringing sound came out—"then it is improperly sealed. But this jar is properly sealed. You can tell when you unscrew it." She twisted the lid, and there was a slight hiss and then the familiar pop of a lid unsealing. "See? Easy to tell."

"And if a jar is sealed properly, there's no chance of bacteria getting in, right?" Cheryl asked.

"That is right. That is the point of the whole process," Naomi said.

Cheryl thought about this for a moment. It made sense. And Kathy Kimble would certainly know something was wrong with any jar that didn't sound right when it opened. She couldn't be so certain about the tourist woman, but surely the jam would have tasted funny if it had spoiled.

But then, Ben hadn't suggested that the jam might have spoiled. He had suggested that it seemed like the tourist woman had ingested poison somehow. Cheryl thought for a moment and considered how to phrase this next part carefully.

"Is there any chance something could have gotten into your jam without you realizing it?"

Naomi took a sip of her tea and waited a moment before answering. "Do you mean, could rat poison have gotten into my jam?"

Cheryl nodded hesitantly.

"I do not see how." Naomi shrugged. "We do have rat poison in the basement, but I did not put it in my jam. And if the jars were sealed..." She let her voice trail off.

Cheryl understood. If the jars were sealed, then rat poison would have had to have been added to the jam while she was making it, and she hadn't done that.

"Could the jars have been opened and resealed after poison was added?" Cheryl asked.

Naomi shrugged. "Technically it is possible. You can reseal a jar that has not sealed properly. But to do that, you must reprocess the jar, which means to boil it in a pot of water for quite a while. And if you did that, the label would come off." Naomi touched the white sticker she handwrote for each jar.

The label had definitely been there on the jar she'd sold at the shop, the jar the man brought to her.

"I'm sure they'll figure out it was something else entirely very soon," Cheryl said quickly.

Naomi nodded. "I just hope Kathy and this tourist woman are all right."

"I am sure they will be." Cheryl spooned up the rest of the soup. "And please know that I believe you, 100 percent, that your jam had nothing to do with the women getting sick. I was asking the questions so we could understand how to rule the jam out. And I think you have just done so."

"Thank you, Cheryl," Naomi said. But something in her face was troubled. Cheryl wanted to say more, to apologize for even asking the questions, but just then the back door opened, and Naomi's husband Seth came in, followed by twenty-year-old Eli, and Levi. Cheryl's heart pounded when she saw Levi, and he flashed her a smile.

The men were chattering in Pennsylvania Dutch as they walked in, but Naomi stopped them and ordered them back to the doorway to remove their work boots and coats before they came any farther. Though she said it all in Pennsylvania Dutch, Cheryl understood the message loud and clear, as did the men. Naomi sprang up and set the kettle on to boil. A moment later, they came back into the room in just their indoor clothes—dark pants, white shirts, suspenders, warm socks—and moved in toward the kitchen. Levi's cheeks were pink from the cold, and he looked healthy and strong.

"Hello, Cheryl," Levi said, meeting and catching her eye. Eli and Seth also said hi, but it was Levi who had Cheryl's attention.

"I am so ready for this winter to be over," Eli said as he reached into the propane-powered refrigerator and took out a glass jar of milk. Eli had dark hair, like Naomi, and though he was typically quiet, he had a jovial personality, and he brought a lot of humor and life to the Miller household. Levi, by contrast, took after his mother, who had passed away when he was a child, and he had light hair and a more reserved way of approaching the world.

"Do not wish your life away," Seth said mildly. "It will be over soon enough as it is."

Cheryl had gotten used to what she would have thought was morbid talk. She understood now that Seth was just not afraid to speak of the things most people preferred to not think about.

"It does seem to get colder every year," Levi said. "And the snow somehow gets worse."

"It is February. You cannot complain about snow in February," Seth said. "That is like complaining about the moon at night."

"Some nights I would like the moon to shine a little less brightly," Levi said with a shrug. "And some days I cannot wait to walk among flowers and eat fresh vegetables from *Maam's* garden and feel the warm sun on my face."

Seth's answer was a grunt.

"Maybe I will move to Florida." Eli poured the milk into a tall glass. "I hear Pinecraft is lovely. Caleb is smart to be visiting friends down there right now."

Cheryl recognized the name of a popular Amish vacation destination along Florida's west coast.

"You go right ahead and move," Naomi said mildly. She set tea bags into mugs for her husband and sons. "Just make sure you do your chores first."

"What about you, Cheryl?" Levi asked. For a moment she was startled. She so enjoyed seeing the family interact that she was almost surprised to be asked to join in. But she was grateful to be included.

"I can't help wishing for spring either," Cheryl said. "Winter is beautiful in its own way, but it doesn't compare to spring, with all the flowers blooming and the trees budding." She smiled. "And, if I'm honest, I'm kind of over the snow."

"See?" Eli said, like she had just proven some important point.

"You know, on the way over here I was thinking about how I used to go skiing at this time of year," Cheryl said. "That helped make winter bearable. But there isn't a ski resort around here, is there?" There were plenty of small hills in the rolling countryside of Tuscarawas County, but nothing for hundreds of miles that counted as a mountain.

All four of the Millers in the room stared at her like she was speaking a foreign language. The kettle started whistling, and Naomi turned the stove off, but still no one spoke. Levi looked confused, while Seth's brow was furrowed.

"I take it you don't ski?" Cheryl said, letting out a small laugh as she imagined stoic Seth racing down the mountain in his hat and suspenders, his coat flying back behind him. She tried to imagine him staying at one of the sleek resorts near the mountains.

"We have never been," Levi said. "Though I have always thought it looks like fun."

"As you said, there is not really any place to try it out around here," Naomi said, gesturing toward the window. "And skiing is quite expensive, is it not?"

True, when you factored in all the gear you had to wear, as well as the ski rentals and lift pass and hotel, it really could add up quickly. But the Millers weren't averse to spending money, at least not on things they thought were worthwhile.

"And it is dangerous," Seth added. "If *Gott* intended us to fly, He would have given us wings."

Cheryl wasn't sure Seth understood the mechanics of skiing, but she decided not to argue that point.

"Plus, our community is suspicious of anything that sounds like too much fun," Eli said. He finished his milk and set the glass down.

Seth said something Cheryl didn't understand in Pennsylvania Dutch, and Eli looked a bit chastised. A bit, but not too much.

"Oh, are there rules against skiing?" Cheryl asked. It seemed odd, but then she was surprised by some of the things there were rules about.

"Oh no, nothing like that," Naomi said. She poured hot water into each of the mugs, and then she set the kettle back on the stove. "It is just not something we really do."

"Maybe it is time to change that." Levi gave Cheryl a sly smile.

This time Naomi said something in Pennsylvania Dutch, but Levi didn't seem to hear her.

"Yes, that sounds like a great idea," Eli said, looking toward Cheryl. "Cheryl, could you teach us?"

Cheryl looked from Eli to Levi and then to Naomi and Seth. The last place she wanted to be was in the middle of a family disagreement. She thought quickly.

Naomi sighed and said something to Seth as she handed him a mug of tea. He thought for a minute and answered her, and Naomi gave Cheryl a small, tentative nod.

"Yes, Cheryl, could you teach us to ski?" Levi's blue eyes shone.

Cheryl would have had a hard time saying no to anything Levi asked.

"Well, if you were going to ski, cross-country skiing might be a better place to start," Cheryl said as diplomatically as she could. She only had downhill skis, but they would suffice for teaching cross-country, at least at first. "That is much cheaper, since you can do it anywhere. You could learn it right here on your farm. And it doesn't involve going down steep mountains," she said, looking at Seth. "It's just strapping on a pair of skis and exploring the world in winter."

Eli looked dubious. "It is like going for a walk, but with skis?"

"No, it's much more fun than that," Cheryl said. "It's . . ." She tried to think of how to describe the feeling of gliding through a quiet forest in the dead of winter. *Beautiful* didn't cut it, nor did *majestic*. "It's almost spiritual, really."

That remark earned her dubious looks from all but Naomi, who seemed to be brightening to the idea.

"It's really fun, I promise," Cheryl said. "And you have to learn the basics that you'd need on a mountain anyway. Once you master cross-country, you could try downhill at some later point," she said, trying to mollify everyone in the room.

Cheryl wasn't at all sure how she had gotten in this position. But she had to admit that the idea of teaching Levi and his brother to ski sounded fun, and it might make the rest of winter seem a bit more bearable. And it wouldn't hurt that it would mean more time with Levi. A vision of the two of them skiing side by side through quiet farmland under a wintry moon filled her mind.

"So," Levi said, holding the steaming mug of tea Naomi had handed him. He gave her a knowing grin. "When will you be teaching Eli and me to ski?"

Cheryl looked around the room. Naomi's head was inclined, and she was looking at her husband. Eli and Levi were both smiling broadly. They all turned to look at Seth, who was gazing down at the table. Cheryl didn't want to move forward without his blessing.

Finally, with everyone in the room watching him, Seth muttered something Cheryl didn't understand. But judging by the reactions of Eli and Levi, it was something akin to permission.

"How about tomorrow?" Eli said. She'd rarely seen him this excited about anything.

Cheryl thought quickly. She knew she had a couple of pairs of skis buried in Aunt Mitzi's basement somewhere.

"It might take me a day or so to find everything. How about Wednesday?"

"Wednesday it is," Levi said, holding her gaze, a wide smile on his face.

To see that smile, Cheryl would do just about anything. She nodded. This was going to be fun.

CHAPTER THREE

Cheryl checked her e-mail as she ate breakfast the next morning, and she was delighted to see a message from Aunt Mitzi. She opened it eagerly. Cheryl loved to hear about her aunt's life in Papua New Guinea, and updates from her were always such a treat.

Cheryl,

I've been thinking about you and my Sugarcreek community, so I thought I'd drop you a line to say hello. It is warm here, as always. It was 88 degrees, and I sat outside in shirtsleeves while I did my devotions this morning. It feels almost wrong to be wearing shorts in February. I am grateful God didn't call me to be a missionary somewhere like Greenland or Siberia. I don't think I would fare so well there.

Though I do have to confess, seeing pictures my friends from back home have been posting on Facebook, I kind of miss the snow. Does that make me seem ungrateful? These old bones really are thankful most of the time for the warmth, but there's something about the way the world looks clean and peaceful blanketed in snow that I find myself missing.

In any case, our work here is going well. I have become
close to a neighbor who seems interested in hearing more
about Jesus every day, and I would be grateful for your
prayers about her.

How are things with Levi? Have the two of you spoken
any more about what the future could look like? I pray
every day that the Lord will direct your paths.

Much love,

Aunt Mitzi

Cheryl read through the message once, quickly, and then again,
savoring the words, and then she sat back. She didn't know what to
say about her and Levi, except that they were still trying to figure
things out. They were both interested in pursuing a relationship,
but sometimes the hurdles to that seemed too high. Levi would
have to leave the Amish, breaking a vow he'd made to God and his
community, to marry Cheryl, and they were still working out
whether that was something they could or would pursue.

Cheryl took a sip of her coffee and decided she would think
more about how to respond to Aunt Mitzi's question later.

Cheryl leaned back in her chair and stretched her legs out in
front of her. She should get going. She had to finish getting ready
before going in to open up the Swiss Miss. She pushed herself up
and took one last gulp of her coffee and then carried her dishes to
the sink. As she set the dish down, she glanced out the window.
The ground was coated with a fresh layer of white powder, and the
sky was a steely gray that promised more snow was on the way.

Ugh. They had plenty of snow here. If only there were some way to share it with Aunt Mitzi, Cheryl thought, laughing. They had plenty to share.

A little while later, the lights of the Swiss Miss were on and the little stove by the door was pumping out heat as fast as it could. Cheryl tied a red apron around her waist, and she looked around the little shop. It was warm and cozy in here; all in all, not a bad place to be on a raw, gray day like today. She still had a few minutes before the shop officially opened. After she set out more soap from the storage room, she called about getting more cheese. Then she looked around and started straightening shelves. The soaps looked nice, as did the jams.

She went over to the shelves where the wooden toys were kept. In addition to hand-carved whistles, animals, and small replicas of buggies, Cheryl had recently started stocking handmade snow globes, made by an Amish man who had just moved his family into the area. When he had first come in and asked her to stock his snow globes, Cheryl hadn't been very interested, but then he'd pulled one out of his bag, and she'd been astounded. The glass ball was hand-blown, and he carved the base himself too. But it was the scenes inside the snow globes that had so thrilled her. He had carved and painted miniscule but beautifully detailed scenes. One was an Amish farm, complete with cows in the fields and Amish clothing on the clothesline. One showed a buggy driving down a peaceful country lane, surrounded by ripening corn. One was even a miniature version of the main street of Sugarcreek, with the businesses all represented by hand-carved wooden buildings. Cheryl couldn't imagine how much work had gone into each of these snow globes, and they were stunning.

She picked up the farm one now and turned it upside down. White flakes of "snow" fell gently, blanketing the barn and farmland in white. The pieces were each unique, and they were a bit more pricey than most of the merchandise in the shop, but Cheryl felt they were worth it. Carefully, she set the snow globe back on the shelf and straightened the other toys.

The front door of the shop blew open, and Ben Vogel stepped inside, a Swiss Miss shopping bag dangling from his arm. He pulled the door closed, but not before flakes of snow blew in.

"It's a nasty day out there," Ben said, shaking himself off. "But it feels wonderful in here." He laughed as the lenses of his glasses fogged up, and he took them off and started toward the counter.

"Hello, Ben," Cheryl said, trying to smile, though her heart was in her throat. The bag he had hooked over his arm was the same shopping bag she'd given him with the jam yesterday. Was there any way he had the results from his friend's lab already?

But even if he did, it would only prove that the jam was not responsible, she reminded herself. Still, she couldn't deny that she was nervous.

"Hi, Cheryl. I wanted to talk to you right away."

Cheryl directed him toward the back of the shop, and he followed her toward the counter. "Did you get the test results back already?"

"Yes." Ben set the shopping bag on the counter and pulled his arm free from the handles. "That's why I rushed over here this morning. I took the jar to my friend's lab last night, and he stayed late to run a few tests after hours for me."

"That was very nice of him," Cheryl said.

"He's an old friend from medical school. He was glad to do it," Ben said.

Cheryl held her breath, waiting for Ben to go on.

"I had him test for the presence of various chemical compounds, just to see what, if anything, turned up."

"And did anything?"

Ben hesitated for a moment and then nodded. "He could tell pretty quickly that there was more than just fruit and sugar in the jam."

Cheryl felt her heart sink.

"After he ran a few tests, he discovered a number of chemicals in the jam. He detected the presence of an anticoagulant, as well as calciferols and zinc phosphide."

Cheryl looked at him blankly. Was he speaking a foreign language?

"In short, those are all chemical compounds that would be found in a commercially prepared rat poison."

Ah. Cheryl understood that bit loud and clear.

"Are you sure?" Her mind reeled. It wasn't possible. How would rat poison have ended up in Naomi's strawberry jam?

"I'm afraid it's true," Ben said sheepishly. "I know it's not what you wanted to hear, but I thought it would be important to know.

You'll probably want to stop selling the jam until you figure out more of what happened." He nodded toward the shelf where the jars of jam were displayed.

Goodness. Yes, she would pull the jars off the shelf right away. But first... She shook her head. Naomi didn't put the poison in her jam. Cheryl was certain about that. But then how did it get there?

"Thank you, Ben," Cheryl said, taking a deep breath. "I don't know how to thank you enough."

"It's not a problem. I just hope the woman is okay. Have you heard how she's doing?"

Cheryl shook her head. "I should probably call the bed-and-breakfast and find out." Then she remembered something. "Kathy Kimble got sick too. She ate some of Naomi's jam as well."

"Oh dear." Ben's eyes widened. "How is she doing?"

Cheryl shook her head. "I had it on my list to check in today." She thought for a moment more. "She ate jam from her shop, not from here."

"Oh." Ben pushed his glasses up. "Which means the jam with the poison isn't just jam from your shop."

"And which also means we should probably warn everyone not to use Naomi's jam," Cheryl said. She had a sick feeling in her gut. Her friend would be heartbroken. Heartbroken and confused, no doubt. Not to mention the financial hit she'd take, having her jam pulled from shelves all over town.

"I'm so sorry, Cheryl," Ben said. "Please let me know if there's anything I can do to help with all of this."

"You have nothing to be sorry for," Cheryl said. "Thank goodness for your help. Now we know to pull the jam, at least until we know more about how this happened and how many jars are affected."

Ben nodded, his look downcast, and then he said good-bye and turned and headed out the door. Cheryl decided to try calling Naomi to tell her the news, but the phone at the Millers' house was in a phone shanty out by the road, and it rang and rang before being picked up by the answering machine. There probably weren't too many people hanging out in the driveway to hear the phone ring on a day like today. And their record in picking up messages was spotty at best. Her Amish friends, unlike most other people she knew, were not exactly addicted to their phones. Well, she would go out to see Naomi as soon as she could.

First, though, she went around the counter, ducked into the back room, and dug a cardboard box out of the closet. Then she went back into the main part of the shop and removed the jars of Naomi's jam off the shelves, one at a time. She pulled off the strawberry jam first, and then the blueberry, blueberry peach, and apricot. There was a special winter gooseberry jam as well, and there were even a few left from the apple-cranberry batch Naomi had made for the holidays. There hadn't been any problems with any of these other kinds, Cheryl thought. But she knew she should take them all off, just to be safe. It was such a shame. The jars, glistening with ripe fruit, were beautiful, and she knew from experience that they were all delicious.

Once she'd taken all the jam down, the shelf looked bare. Well, hopefully it would only be for a short time. Just until they got this sorted out, which would hopefully be very soon. Then she called the Honey Bee. Heather answered and thanked Cheryl again for her help the previous night. She confirmed that Kathy was still in the hospital and that Heather was opening up on her own for the day. She was shocked when Cheryl told her about the poison in the jam, and she promised to take all of Naomi's jam out of their kitchen until they found out more.

After that, Cheryl was anxious to do more. The shop was quiet, so she called Kathy Kimble's cell phone next. The call rang and rang and then went to her voice mail. Cheryl left a message wishing her the best, and then she hung up. She didn't have Kathy's husband Keith's phone number. Well, if she didn't hear back from Kathy, she would stop by the hospital later today.

Then Cheryl sat down at the computer at the counter and pulled up a browser window. She typed in the words *rat poison* and read the pages that came up. It was nasty stuff, she discovered. It was generally described as having a sweet taste, which was why children often ingested it when they found it. A small amount could kill animals and even humans if they weren't treated right away, though thankfully that typically required a larger dose. It seemed most rat poisons were made from a number of different chemicals that acted in different ways to kill. Nausea and vomiting were early symptoms, though other symptoms, like bleeding and bruising, could take longer to appear. The main ingredient in most rat poisons was an anticoagulant, or blood thinner, that led to internal bleeding. The zinc phosphide in the poison could lead to cardiopulmonary complications, as well as liver failure. She couldn't believe this horrible stuff had actually found its way into Naomi's jam.

A few customers came in, braving the raw day, and Cheryl spent a few minutes helping them select wooden toys for their grandchildren. They liked the snow globes, but the price was a bit high for what they were looking for, and they ended up with sets of miniature farm animals. After they paid, they didn't linger, and soon the store was quiet again. Cheryl tried the Miller phone line again, but no one picked up. She was going crazy, desperate to talk to Naomi. It was times like these that she really hated the whole no-cell-phones rule. Lydia Troyer was not scheduled to come in today. When Esther arrived, Cheryl decided, she would go by the farm and talk to Naomi directly.

Another set of customers came in from a tour group that had just descended upon Sugarcreek, and as Cheryl helped them pick out souvenirs, Cheryl chatted with them about where they were from and why they had chosen a snowy day in February to see the Amish town. It was hardly prime tourist season, but everything from the bus to the hotels was cheaper this way, they told her. When they had all gone, Cheryl heard the door open, and she looked up anxiously, expecting to see Esther Miller step in, but she was pleased to see that it was Naomi.

"Naomi! You came to town today?"

Her friend nodded and shoved the door closed against the howling wind. She pulled off her gloves and slipped off her cloak and paused for a moment, enjoying the heat that came from the stove. Then she hung up her cloak on the hooks by the door, turned, and started to walk toward Cheryl, who waited at the back of the store.

"Hannah Gingerich needed to come into Hoffman's Furniture to get a new crib because they have twins coming in a few weeks and they only have one crib. She hired Jessica Stockton to drive her to town," Naomi said. "And she asked if I wanted to share a ride in with her. I had a few errands to run in town, and she said we could go by the grocery store too. Since I needed to stock up on a few things, it made sense to come in."

Ah. Jessica Stockton was a Yoder Toter, a driver hired to bring Amish folks around in her big van when the distance was deemed too far—or the weather too nasty—for Amish horses to make the trip.

"Esther came with me, and she will be here for her shift shortly. But first she wanted to chat with a few of the girls at Yoder's Corner," Naomi said, gesturing toward the restaurant a few doors down from the shop. Waitressing there was a popular job for Amish girls Esther's age.

Esther was such an asset to the store, she wished the girl could work more hours.

"It is nice to get out and go into town every once in a while," Naomi said. "But I also wanted to see if you had heard anything more about that tourist woman or about Kathy Kimble."

"Well, I'm glad you came in because I've been trying to get ahold of you about that," Cheryl said.

"Oh?" Naomi said. She looked around and noticed the empty shelf where her jam was usually displayed. "Oh no, Cheryl... It isn't..." She couldn't even seem to figure out how to finish the sentence.

"Ben Vogel came in here this morning," Cheryl started. She pointed to the jar of jam he'd tested, which she'd moved to the side of the counter, next to the cash register. "And he told me that the tests had come back positive. There was rat poison in that jar of jam."

Naomi gasped, and then she shook her head. "Are you certain?"

"I'm afraid that's what Ben said," Cheryl said.

Naomi didn't say anything for a moment. "But how is that possible? Cheryl, I promise you, I did not put poison in the jam."

"I know you didn't," Cheryl said.

Naomi's face had gone white. She leaned against the counter and placed her hands on the wooden surface, bracing herself.

"That's why I wanted to talk to you." Cheryl patted Naomi's arm. "I want to figure out how it got there."

"I do not..." Naomi shook her head again. Cheryl hopped up and carried a stool around to the far side of the counter and gestured for Naomi to sit. Slowly, Naomi lowered herself down.

"I know you didn't do this, Naomi. Which means someone else did." Cheryl had been thinking about this since Ben had told her the verdict, and she'd already decided she wanted to help if she could. But she wasn't the only one who should be looking into this. "The first thing you should probably do is call the police."

"Oh, Cheryl, I do not know."

"Someone poisoned your jam. That's a crime," Cheryl continued. "Telling the police will not only get them to start looking for whoever did this, but it will also make it clear to them that you're blameless."

"But if they ask, I can simply tell them I did not do it."

"Maybe." Sometimes Naomi was blessedly naive when it came to things like how the police operated. But Cheryl tried to tread carefully. She knew that the Amish did not like to involve the police in their affairs unless it was absolutely necessary. She could see that Naomi was not convinced yet. Understandably enough, she supposed. Naomi had just been blindsided by the fact that her jam was tainted. She might need a few minutes to come around to the idea of the police.

"Okay, we can talk about the police again later. I do think they need to know what's happened, but in the meantime, let's see what we can figure out on our own."

Naomi nodded, but she still seemed dazed. Cheryl waited a moment. Then she continued.

"I'm trying to understand how the poison could have gotten into the jars," Cheryl said. "If I understand the process correctly, the seal would have been broken if someone had messed with the jam after you put it in the jar, right?"

She grabbed the jar Ben had brought back and set it down on the counter between them, and then she sat down on another stool. Naomi nodded, her eyes wide. Cheryl couldn't be positive that the seal hadn't been broken on the jar that the tourist had opened, but Cheryl was certain that Kathy knew enough not to eat from a jar that didn't sound right when she opened it.

"Then we need to figure out how the poison got into your jam *before* you sealed the jar," Cheryl said. Naomi nodded without a word. "Do you have any idea how to figure out when you made this particular batch of jam?" Cheryl asked.

"Yes." Naomi pulled the jar closer to her and squinted at the handwritten label. She paused for just a moment, tilted her head, and then shook it ever so slightly. "See here?" She pointed to a line of text Cheryl had seen a thousand times on Naomi's jam jars, but never looked at properly. She looked at it now. Naomi had written *Best before January 15* of the following year.

"The jam will last for a good while on a shelf, but I do not think it will last forever, so I have been adding this date to give people a guideline for when to finish the jam," Naomi said. "I do not want it to sit on their shelves for years, and then they open it to discover it has gone bad and blame me."

Cheryl nodded. Putting an expiration date on the jam made sense to her. Fortunately, the jam never sat on her shelves long enough that she'd ever had to rotate stock out based on that date.

"I always put this date as a year from the day I make it," Naomi said. "So I made the jam in this jar on January 15 of this year." She bit her lip and paused for a moment, thinking. "Which makes sense. I do remember that I did make jam on that day. I made a big batch, in fact. It was because the freezer was broken."

Cheryl wrinkled her brow. She'd been following Naomi up to that point.

Seeing her confusion, Naomi continued. "I keep a propane-powered freezer in the basement. In it, I keep lots of things, like meat and leftovers when I make too much, as well as berries from the garden that I do not use right away."

"Got it." Cheryl nodded. That made sense.

"Elizabeth had noticed on that morning that the freezer was not working right, so I had called a repairman. But meanwhile, the food inside the freezer was spoiling. We put the meat outside in the snow," Naomi said with a grin. "But I decided to use up the strawberries before they could go bad by making jam."

"Great," Cheryl said. "So now we know when the jam was made. Now we just need to figure out who all was around the day you were making the jam. That will give us the list of suspects for who could have tampered with the jam." She grabbed a stray bit of paper and pen from next to the register, ready to write down the names.

"Okay," Naomi said, dubiously. "Well, I guess Seth, Caleb, Eli, Levi, Elizabeth, and Esther were around."

Cheryl's pen hovered over the paper. Technically, they should all be considered suspects, but she had a hard time imagining that any of them had actually poisoned Naomi's jam.

"Who else?" Cheryl said without writing down their names.

Naomi thought for a moment. "The repairman came by that day. I know that."

"Good. Who was he?"

"I do not remember his name. We found him in the phone book. We have not used him before, but the man we usually call when an appliance goes haywire was away that day. We could not wait for him to get back, so we found this man. I liked the neat star in his ad."

Cheryl wrote down: "repairman with star in his ad."

"What was he like?" Cheryl asked.

Naomi thought for a moment. "He was…well, gruff, maybe. He was not the most friendly man. But he showed up on time and he fixed our freezer quickly and cheaply. I do not remember much else about him, I'm afraid."

Cheryl wrote the facts down. "When he was fixing the freezer, was he left alone in the basement at any point?"

Naomi nodded. "Sure. We did not stay down there with him while he worked."

"And the basement is where you keep the rat poison, right?"

"Ye…es," Naomi said carefully. "I guess it is possible he took some of the poison." She thought for a minute. "But I was already working on the jam by the time he arrived. So he would have had to bring the poison upstairs and put it into the cooking jam at some point without me noticing."

That part complicated her theory, she supposed, but he was still someone she needed to look into, for certain.

"About what time did you start cooking the jam?" Cheryl asked.

"I started warming the berries around ten that morning, I guess," Naomi said after a short pause. "And I did not finish sealing all the jars until midafternoon, I think."

"And what time did the repairman get there?"

"I believe it was shortly after eleven," Naomi said. "It was just before Sylvia came over to return the pot she had borrowed. And she ended up staying for lunch because Martha was hungry, so I know she came over around then."

"Sylvia..." Cheryl thought for a moment. "Which Sylvia?"

Naomi laughed. It was a common name in their community. "My cousin Sylvia. Her son is Jonas?"

"Ah." Cheryl knew now. She had met Sylvia the previous year when there had been a fund-raiser for her son Jonas, who had been diagnosed with diabetes. "How is Jonas doing?"

"Much better," Naomi said. "In fact, Sylvia had borrowed the pot to make a large batch of noodles for a gathering to celebrate Jonas's birthday."

"I'm so glad to hear it." Cheryl shifted on the stool. "You said she and Martha stayed for lunch?"

"Yes. Martha is her daughter. She just turned four, and she was getting cranky because she hadn't eaten, so they had sandwiches."

"So Sylvia was in the kitchen? Where the jam was?"

Naomi shook her head. "There is no way my cousin put rat poison in my jam. It is not possible."

Cheryl had enough experience helping with mysteries to know that nothing was impossible, but it wouldn't help to say so now. From what she could tell, Naomi and her cousin got along swimmingly, and she couldn't see what motive Sylvia would have for tampering with the jam.

The door of the store whooshed open, and two older women in matching cat sweatshirts came in. Cheryl asked if they needed help, but they indicated they were just browsing, so she turned back to Naomi. Cheryl thought for a moment. "What about Martha?"

Naomi gave her a strange look. "You think a four-year-old poisoned my jam?"

"I'm just trying to think of every possibility," Cheryl said. "Did Martha go into the kitchen at any point?"

"Yes, she wanted to help, so she brought me the pectin, and then she helped stir the jam as it was cooling and...," Naomi said, then seemed to realize what she'd said and shook her head. "I know what you are thinking, but there is no way. She is the sweetest, most helpful child."

"I'm not suggesting she did anything on purpose. I'm only trying to see if there is any chance an accident was made," Cheryl said soothingly. "You said she brought you the pectin. Where is the pectin kept?"

Naomi hesitated and then said, "The basement. But there is no way..." Slowly, her voice trailed off.

"What is it?"

"Oh, Cheryl, I have just remembered that she brought the pectin up in a small dish."

Cheryl's mind filled in the holes.

"Meaning you didn't see the container she got it from, right?"

Naomi nodded, her eyes wide.

"What does pectin look like?" Cheryl asked.

Again, Naomi hesitated, and then she said, "It is a fine white powder."

"Much like rat poison?"

Naomi nodded.

She hated to say this next part, but she knew she had to. "Is there any chance Martha might have mistaken one for the other?"

"I do not see how," Naomi said. "They are kept on opposite sides of the basement. The pectin is with my jam supplies, and the poison is on the far side. And the boxes they come in are clearly marked. But…" Her voice broke off. "But of course, Martha cannot read."

"The rat poison isn't locked up in any way?" Cheryl asked. Could Naomi really keep it on a low shelf where a child could get it?

Naomi shook her head. "When the kids were little, we were more careful, but now…"

Her youngest child was seventeen and very responsible. They didn't need to worry about such things anymore.

"How much white powder did she bring up?" Cheryl asked.

"Not much. Maybe a cup. Even for a large batch of jam, you only need a few tablespoons of pectin."

She didn't say the obvious follow-up: that only a few tablespoons of rat poison would be enough to cause serious illness.

"Oh dear," Naomi said, her face suddenly white. "Cheryl, you do not really think…there is not any way…"

"I don't know," Cheryl said. If she was honest, it did seem like a possibility. A four-year-old could easily have mixed up one powder for another, she thought. "If there was a mix-up, it was clearly an accident. But we'll find out. Maybe we could talk to Sylvia and see what she remembers about that day?"

"That is not a bad idea," Naomi said.

"Was there anyone else?" Cheryl asked.

Naomi closed her eyes and thought for a moment. "I do not remember," she finally said. "It was a very ordinary day. I did not make special note of who came and went because there was nothing odd about it to me."

Cheryl understood. Unless you had some reason to remember the details of a particular day, it could be hard to remember details after the fact. One day was often much like any other. Which was fine until you needed to remember the details of any one in particular.

The door opened again, and this time Cheryl turned around and saw Esther come inside the shop. Naomi looked up and said something to her daughter in Pennsylvania Dutch, and Esther nodded and shoved the door closed. She came toward the counter.

"How is Sarah Ann?" Naomi said.

"She is very much looking forward to the Singing this weekend because John has promised to give her a ride home," Esther said, nodding at her mother. Then she went around the counter and pulled a red apron off the hook in the back room. Cheryl didn't know who John and Sarah Ann were, but she knew enough about teenagers to understand the gist of what was going on. Since she'd moved to the area, she'd discovered that Amish teens were just like other teenagers, though they expressed it differently.

"How is it going here?" Esther asked, reaching back to tie the apron behind her back.

The two customers waved good-bye and headed out, and the door fell closed behind them. The shop was empty once more.

Naomi quickly filled her in on what Cheryl had told her and what they were doing, and Esther's mouth fell open.

"You cannot be serious," Esther said. "But who would do such a terrible thing?"

"That's what we're trying to figure out," Cheryl said. "We're trying to figure out everyone who had the opportunity to slip the poison into the jam the day your mother made it."

"You got the repairman?" Esther said. "He was down in the basement a long time. He could have taken some of the poison and brought it up and dumped it in the jam when no one was looking."

Cheryl nodded. "And your cousin, Sylvia, and her daughter, Martha."

"What about Andy?" she said.

"Andy?" It took Naomi a few seconds, but then she nodded. "Was that the day Andy came?"

"Who is Andy?" Cheryl asked.

"Andy Glick. He is a friend of Eli's," Naomi said. She seemed to be trying to decide whether to say anything more.

"Maam doesn't like him," Esther said.

"Ah." That explained Naomi's reaction. "Why not?"

"It is not that I do not *like* him," Naomi said. "It is just that I do not think he is a very good influence on Eli."

"And you would rather he did not hang around him," Esther said.

Naomi did not deny it. "Of course I do not want a boy who is always in trouble to be around my son, trying to convince him to do bad things. But that does not mean I do not like him."

Esther looked at Cheryl. "She does not like him," she said. Cheryl had to laugh. Again, teenagers were the same, no matter the culture.

"What sort of trouble does he get into?" Cheryl asked.

"Oh, the usual." Esther laughed. "Buggy racing. Mixing up men's hats during worship. Trying to get his friends' horses to eat ice cream."

Cheryl laughed. Okay, maybe all teenagers weren't *exactly* the same.

"It is more than that," Naomi said, a touch of defensiveness in her voice. "He had been disciplined by the bishop for stealing."

"He took Marlin Burkholder's new buggy for a spin during a Singing one time. But he brought it back."

"He changed the answering machine message in the Kauffmans' phone shanty to say that callers had reached Pizza Hut."

"You would be surprised how many people then left orders for pizza," Esther said with a big smile on her face.

"It sounds like Andy is into practical jokes," Cheryl said.

"Yes, he thinks of himself as a jokester," Naomi said.

"And he was there the day you made the jam?"

"He came over after lunch," Esther volunteered. "He wanted Eli to come with him to check out a horse he wanted to buy. I remember that he kept pretending to stick his fingers into the jam while it was cooling in the jars."

"He did not really touch the jam, I hope?" Naomi asked, a look of disgust crossing her features.

"No, Eli told him to knock it off," Esther said. "And Eli was working on repairing the door on Sugar's stall in the barn with *Daed*, so he told Andy he couldn't go, and then Andy left."

Cheryl tried to phrase this next bit carefully. "Do you think there's any chance Andy could have thought it was a funny joke to do more than pretend to touch the jam?"

Naomi and Esther looked at each other, and Esther sighed.

"I do not know," Esther finally said. "I guess it is possible."

"I do not want to think that someone from our community could have done something like this," Naomi said. "But I cannot say for sure that he would not."

Cheryl looked down at her paper and wrote his name on her list.

"Can you think of anyone else?" Both Naomi and Esther shook their heads.

"Not anyone other than the family," Naomi said. Cheryl wouldn't insult her by asking if any member of the Miller family could have been responsible. Cheryl couldn't imagine sweet Elizabeth or stoic Seth dumping rat poison into Naomi's jam.

Cheryl tapped her pen against the counter, and she had a thought. "How long had the berries been in your freezer?"

Naomi shrugged. "Since last summer, I suppose. June, most likely."

"Is there any chance someone could have tampered with the berries in that time?"

Naomi blew out a breath. "I suppose it is possible," she said reluctantly. "But I would not have any idea how to list all the people who might have been in our basement since June. We hosted church in October, which means that everyone in the district has been in our house."

Cheryl nodded. She knew that the Amish community did not have a church building, but members took turns hosting church in their homes. Cheryl had seen how the Millers would go into a cleaning frenzy, dusting their house from top to bottom, and then move their furniture outside and set up long rows of wooden benches in the living room.

"And then when you think about all the guests and family who have visited us..." Her voice trailed off. "I do not think it is possible to make a list of everyone who could have had access to our basement, and I also do not believe that anyone from our community would have done such a thing."

Cheryl could see the logic of what she was saying, except for one fatal flaw: someone *had* done such a thing. She didn't know who it had been yet, but chances were good, if Cheryl's list could be believed, that it had been someone from their community who had messed with her jam, intentionally or not. But Cheryl knew better than to say that. Besides, it did seem like a near-impossible task trying to track down everyone who could have been in the Millers' basement since June.

"How many jars did you make?" Cheryl asked.

Naomi let out a long breath. "It was a large batch. I was trying to use up the fruit before it went bad. I believe I probably made four dozen jars or so that day."

Cheryl didn't know how Naomi managed the scope of a project like that, especially with a family to feed and a farm and petting zoo to run.

"And how many of the jars from that batch have you sold?" Cheryl asked.

"Oh, goodness. Maybe half?" Naomi sighed. "I brought a dozen to you, and another dozen to Greta Yoder." Cheryl nodded. She knew they served Naomi's jam at Yoder's Corner. "And I gave one to Kathy as a birthday gift, as well as one to Anna Lapp, along with a pair of knitted booties, when her daughter was born last week," Naomi added. "I think that is all."

"We will need to tell Greta to stop serving the jam right away," Esther said. "I can go over and do that."

"You will stay here at your job, not run off gossiping with your friends," Naomi said. "I will tell Greta. And I will stop by the Lapps' on the way home and tell her not to eat the jam. Goodness, I hope I have not poisoned a new mother."

"I'm sure she's fine," Cheryl said. "And even if for some reason she's eaten some, it is not your fault. We all know you had nothing to do with this."

Naomi just shook her head. "I sure wish we did know who was behind it."

"Well, I am going to do everything I can to figure that out. And, again, I think you should get the police involved so they can start looking into it…"

Naomi shook her head. "No. No police." There was a certainty in her tone that hadn't been there earlier.

"But I really think…"

"We will call them if we need to, but right now we do not. I will not have the police going to talk to my cousin telling her I think she poisoned my jam. I will not do that to Andy Glick's family either. We will figure this out on our own."

Cheryl felt uneasy. She saw now why Naomi did not want to bring the police in, but she still felt that it was the right thing to do.

"Please, Cheryl," Naomi continued. "You must understand why I cannot ask the police to look into this."

Cheryl didn't agree, but she heard pleading in her friend's voice. No, not pleading. Resolve. Naomi had made up her mind. Cheryl realized reluctantly that she needed to respect that. For now at least.

"All right." Cheryl looked down at her list. "Can you remember anything about that repairman? I'd probably start there if we can track him down."

Naomi thought for a moment. "I remember he was big, and, well, I guess you would call him rough around the edges. But as for tracking him down?" She shook her head. "I believe he gave us a receipt. I can look for that. Otherwise, all I remember is that star in the ad in the phone book. I am sorry."

Well, Cheryl could start by looking through the phone book. She could do that without Naomi's help, so she would do that later. But she would need Naomi if she wanted to speak with Sylvia about her daughter, Martha. "If you have some time now, we could try to eliminate one suspect," she said.

Naomi nodded. "Yes. Let us go see my cousin."

Chapter Four

Before Cheryl and Naomi set out to talk to her cousin Sylvia, they called Jessica Stockton to let her know that Naomi wouldn't need a ride home, and they also stopped by Yoder's Corner and explained what had happened to Greta Yoder. Greta was a large, jolly woman who always made customers feel welcome at her restaurant. She was shocked and thankful for the warning, and she immediately had her servers pull all the jars of Naomi's jam from the table and toss them out. It hurt Cheryl's heart to see the jars thrown away like that. There was no way to say how many of the jars from that batch were tainted—it could be just the two they knew about, or it could be all of them. The smart thing to do was be safe and get rid of them all, but she knew it hurt her friend's heart and her pocketbook, as she insisted on repaying Greta for the jars she'd had to throw away. Naomi had offered the same thing to Cheryl, but she had refused.

Now as they drove out past acres of quiet farmland blanketed in a layer of white snow, the only sound was the soft scraping of the wipers against the windshield. Cheryl wanted to probe, to see how Naomi was feeling about all this, but she knew that her friend often held things in. She wasn't one to open up about her feelings. If she wanted to talk about what was going on, she would. Naomi spent most of the ride to Sylvia's gazing silently out the window.

Sylvia's house was smaller than Naomi's, but it was well-kept, and it had cheerful green shutters on the upstairs windows. The red barn on the far side of the field looked picturesque against the stark white snow. Naomi led them up the porch steps and knocked on the front door.

"*Aenti* Naomi," said a small redheaded girl that seemed to be a bit too old to be Martha. Naomi introduced her as Irene, Martha's six-year-old sister. She led them inside and closed the door and showed them to the kitchen, chattering in their dialect the whole time. Then she disappeared up the stairs. In the kitchen, they found Sylvia rolling out a pie crust. Cheryl had yet to walk into an Amish house where there wasn't some delicious treat being made or cooling freshly out of the oven.

"Hello, Naomi. And hello, Cheryl." Her face spread into a smile, and she set down the rolling pin. She wiped her hands on a dish towel and gestured for them to have a seat at the scarred wooden table. "It is so good to see you. Can I get you something warm? Tea? Or hot cocoa? I have some macaroni left over from lunch, if you'd like."

Cheryl realized that she hadn't eaten lunch, but she didn't want to put Sylvia out.

"Some cocoa would be good," Naomi said, and Cheryl said that sounded good to her too. Sylvia pulled a jar of milk out of the refrigerator and poured some into a pot on the stove. She was making it from scratch. But then, Cheryl guessed she shouldn't have expected anything else.

"How is Jonas?" Cheryl asked.

"He is doing very well, thank you. So much better now that he has his insulin pump. He is at school, otherwise I would have him come to see you."

Cheryl had seen Amish schoolchildren walking along the country lanes toward their one-room schoolhouse in all sorts of weather, but she was still impressed that they went on a day like today.

"I'm just glad he's doing better," she said.

"I will tell him you said hello," Sylvia said. "It is wonderful of you to stop by." Her smile was genuine, but Cheryl heard the question in her voice.

"Yes. We are glad to see you, of course. And we had a couple of questions for you," Naomi said. "Do you remember the day a few weeks ago when you came by with Martha?" Naomi asked.

"Yes. That was when I returned the pot, is it not?" Sylvia pulled down a canister of cocoa from a pantry and scooped some into the warming milk. "Martha still has not stopped talking about those cinnamon cookies you gave her that day. She keeps asking me if we can make them. I must get the recipe from you."

"Of course," Naomi said. "I will copy it for you today. But about that day. Do you remember how I was making jam when you stopped by?"

"Of course I remember. Your entire counter was covered with jamming supplies." She added some sugar from a canister on the counter, and she used a wooden spoon to stir the cocoa in the pot. "I felt bad getting in your way when you had so much going on."

"*Ach.* You are never in the way." Naomi shifted in her seat. "But it turns out something strange has happened, and I wondered if you might have seen anything odd that day."

"What is it?" Sylvia turned off the burner and started pouring the hot cocoa into three white mugs.

"Well, it seems that somehow rat poison ended up in the jam," Naomi said.

"What?" Sylvia shrieked, and she dropped the pan on to the stove. Cheryl was grateful that it was now empty. "*Wirklich?*"

She fired questions at Naomi in Pennsylvania Dutch, and Cheryl tried to keep up, but she only understood a bit of what they were saying. However, it was clear that Sylvia was shocked and was trying to figure out how this could be true.

"I am sorry, Cheryl," Naomi said, noticing Cheryl shifting in her chair. "We are being rude. Sylvia was just saying she did not see anything odd while they were there."

"Yes, I am sorry," Sylvia said, setting the mugs of cocoa down on the table. "I was quite surprised, but we will switch to English. Tell me. How can this be?"

"That's what we're hoping to figure out," Cheryl said. "We figure the rat poison had to have been added before the jam jars were sealed, which means sometime that day someone came along and added it. We were hoping you might have seen something."

"No," Sylvia said, shaking her head. "I did not." She wrapped her hands around her mug and thought for a moment. "That was the day you had the repairman in, no? Could he have done it?"

"I'm going to talk to him to see," Cheryl said. She took a sip of the cocoa to give herself time to phrase this next question properly. She couldn't exactly come out and ask if Sylvia's daughter had added the poison herself. "As we were trying to reconstruct the events of the day, Naomi mentioned to me that your daughter, Martha, helped with the jam," Cheryl said brightly.

"Yes..." Sylvia was just a touch guarded, if Cheryl wasn't mistaken.

"She was a big help," Naomi said. "She even went down to the basement for me and got the pectin."

Sylvia nodded, waiting to see what they were getting at.

"The thing is," Cheryl said, taking another sip of the cocoa, "the pectin is down in the basement, and so is the rat poison, and it wouldn't be all that hard to get them confused, especially for a child that age. We wondered if we might be able to talk to Martha, just to ask her what she remembers."

"Oh, Naomi, you do not really think..."

"No, I do not," Naomi said, certainty in her voice. "But we want to talk to her so we can say we asked everyone who was involved that day."

"I do not...," Sylvia started, and then she shook her head. "I cannot imagine she would make a mistake like that. The rat poison is in its box, right? With the skull and crossbones on it?"

Naomi nodded. "And it is kept on the far side of the cellar from the canning supplies. So we do not think it is likely at all, but we wanted to be able to cross her name off the list for sure."

Sylvia nodded, and she stood and moved toward the doorway and called into the next room. Cheryl craned her neck and saw a little girl coloring pictures with crayons at a small desk by the window. She looked up when her mother called, set down her crayon, and obediently came into the kitchen.

"Martha, *kumme*," Sylvia said, indicating she should sit in the empty chair next to Sylvia.

Once again, the girl did exactly as her mother instructed. She was a miniature version of Sylvia, with dark brown hair and big blue eyes and the same upturned nose. She even wore a miniature version of the dark blue dress her mother wore.

Sylvia started speaking to her in a string of words Cheryl couldn't understand.

"Martha does not speak much English yet," Naomi said quietly to Cheryl. Cheryl nodded. She had learned that many Amish children didn't learn much English until they started school, and they spoke Pennsylvania Dutch exclusively until then.

Since she couldn't participate in the questioning, Cheryl watched the girl's body language. She listened, wide-eyed, as her mother asked her questions, and she shook her head gently no. She seemed shy, and she seemed nervous, and when her mother asked her a question, it took her a moment to answer. Naomi then asked her something, and the girl looked around and then down at the table, and then she said something so quietly that Naomi had to ask her to repeat herself. Cheryl couldn't figure out if the girl was just terribly shy or if there was more going on here. Her body language suggested either could be the case.

Naomi and Sylvia talked to her for a few minutes, and then Sylvia dismissed her, and the girl hopped down, gave Cheryl a shy smile, and disappeared back into the next room.

"She says she did not go to the side of the basement where the poison was kept," Naomi said. "I asked her what the package looked like that she took the pectin from, and she described the container perfectly. It comes in a large blue box with fruit on the front, and she described it exactly right."

Cheryl was glad to hear it, though it certainly didn't eliminate the possibility that she had gotten the powder from the wrong container, as far as Cheryl was concerned. But it seemed to satisfy Naomi, and when she pushed herself up, Cheryl couldn't think of a good way to prolong the questioning.

"Thank you for talking with us," Cheryl said, and Sylvia nodded and waved. Naomi and Sylvia chatted for a moment in their dialect, and then Cheryl followed Naomi out of the house and back into the car.

"So?" Cheryl said as they drove toward the Lapp house, so Naomi could warn the new mother not to eat the jam. She would drop Naomi back off at the Miller farm after that. "She says she had nothing to do with it?"

"That is what she says," Naomi said, nodding. The wipers swished across the windshield, sweeping away the faintest flakes of snow. Cheryl couldn't believe Aunt Mitzi missed this. "Martha says that she found the box with the pectin easily because it is the same kind her maam uses. She swears she did not even venture over to the other side of the basement because the 'scary *Englisch* man' was there."

"Scary?"

Naomi shrugged. "He did not seem scary to me. But Martha is a shy child and does not interact with many Englisch. I would guess that any Englisch man would seem scary to her."

Maybe Naomi was right. Or maybe Martha had picked up on something in this repairman that the adults hadn't seen, as children so often did.

Cheryl thought about how to ask this gently. "Do you think there's any chance she's not telling the truth?"

Naomi blew out a breath. "I do not know. She is a good girl and a big help to her maam."

"But surely anyone would insist they weren't responsible in a situation like that," Cheryl said. "How do we know she's telling the truth?"

Naomi didn't say anything for a moment. She adjusted the vent on the dashboard, aligning the slats so the warm air was pointed directly at her. Cheryl knew that Naomi enjoyed riding in her car, especially on bitterly cold days like this. Cheryl had yet to see a buggy with heating vents.

"I do not know," she said. "I cannot prove that she did not make a mistake that day in my basement and that she is not trying to cover it up now. All I can tell you is that I believe she is telling the truth."

Cheryl nodded. There was no way to argue against that. And she wasn't sure she wanted to. Certainly the other names on her list—the teenage Amish prankster and the unknown English repairman—were at least as likely as a confused four-year-old.

But at the same time, the girl's body language could be read to mean that she'd been very uncomfortable with the line of questioning, and Cheryl had met enough four-year-olds to know that the line between truth and fiction was often blurry. They lived in a world where princesses and the Easter Bunny were real, and sometimes it was hard for them to distinguish between what had really happened and what had been their imagination. Sure, Amish kids didn't believe in the Easter Bunny, but she doubted their thought processes were that much different. She wasn't sure Martha's account, as earnest as it seemed, could be trusted, and Cheryl was loathe to eliminate a suspect unless she had firm evidence one way or the other. She wouldn't cross Martha off the list just yet, but she wouldn't tell Naomi that either.

They pulled up to Anna Lapp's house a few minutes later. The girl was young, Cheryl could see, certainly not much older than Esther, and she seemed completely overwhelmed by the baby she held as she answered the door. He was tiny and red-faced, and Cheryl almost couldn't believe that a child that size could be screaming as loudly as he was. Anna, a freckled girl with wild brown curls escaping from her kapp, invited them in, and Cheryl stood around awkwardly as Naomi took the wailing newborn from his mother's arms, calmed him down by making a few soothing noises and swinging him gently, and explained about the jam.

"Oh dear," Anna said. "I have eaten some the past two mornings on my toast."

Naomi blanched, but Cheryl shook her head. "And you have not gotten ill?"

"No," Anna said.

"Then you probably won't," Cheryl said. From what she had read online, it seemed likely the girl would have had some symptoms by now if she was going to get them. "But still, you should probably throw away the jam to be safe."

"Oh, I am so glad you have not gotten sick," Naomi said, her whole body moving as she swung the baby. Was calming a baby like this something some people were born knowing how to do, or did you learn it through experience? Cheryl didn't know, but she hoped that if she ever had children of her own, she would have someone like Naomi around to teach her how to manage it all. "Please throw it out. I will bring you a new jar next time I come out this way."

They chatted for a few minutes, and Cheryl felt silly standing around contributing nothing. They went in and out of their dialect, so she stopped trying to follow the conversation and looked at the sweet little face of the baby Naomi was rocking. As the child settled, Cheryl felt a strange sense of longing. Babies were so tiny, so precious. She hoped she would have a baby of her own one day. She did want one. More than one, in fact. Even one that yelled like this little fellow had. Maybe, if she and Levi were able to . . .

"Thank you so much," Anna said as Naomi handed back a now-sleeping infant. Anna cradled the baby in her arms, and her eyes welled up with tears. "I do not know how you got him to do that, but thank you."

"It gets easier," Naomi said, and the tears spilled over and down Anna's cheeks. "He will sleep more soon, and then it will be much better."

Anna nodded and carefully held the door open for them, being careful not to wake the sleeping child.

Cheryl knew it was silly, but she couldn't help but feel a bit left out. It wasn't that she wished she'd been married and pregnant before her twentieth birthday, like Anna, but sometimes it did seem that she was the only one her age around here who couldn't talk about diapers and nursing with any sort of expertise. And she knew that wasn't likely to change anytime soon, unless… Well, things were not simple between her and Levi.

"Do you have time to make one more stop?" Naomi asked as she buckled her seat belt. She put her hands up against the vents as hot air began to flow out.

"I believe you are only using me for my car's heater," Cheryl said, trying to distract herself from the funk she'd settled into at Anna's house.

"That is certainly not true," Naomi said. "Now, if your car had heated seats, I would be using you for those, without a doubt. But I am only enjoying the heat from these vents while you drive. We could use my buggy next time if you prefer?"

"Let's stick with my car for now," Cheryl said, laughing a bit. A buggy was nice for a relaxing pleasure ride on a nice night or a Sunday drive, but for getting around, Cheryl would stick to her car. She put the car in Reverse, backed up, and pulled out down the slippery driveway, which hadn't been plowed in at least a day and was now coated with a fine layer of fresh snow.

"Where to?" Cheryl asked as she nosed the car out toward the road.

"I thought we could stop by Andy Glick's house to see if he is around," Naomi said.

"Ah. Sure thing," Cheryl said. She remembered his name. He was the Amish jokester.

"Turn left," Naomi said. Cheryl obeyed, pulling out carefully on to the road. "Andy's mother Joyce was a friend of mine in school, so it was natural for Eli and Andy to become friends when they were children," Naomi explained. "Of course as he got older and he started getting into trouble, I began to wish they were not so friendly, but by then it was too late," Naomi said.

"Has he ever been in serious trouble?" Cheryl asked. "Or is it just pranks and that sort of thing?"

"No, he has not gotten in trouble with the police or anything like that." Naomi shook her head. "It is just that he has always been a bit wild, trying to see what he could get away with. And he has not joined the church yet. He still drives his car too fast and is enticed by the world."

Cheryl took this in. She knew that Naomi, like the rest of her community, allowed teens to break the rules during their running-around years, and she had never heard any hint of judgment from Naomi about someone delaying their choice to join the church. She wondered about Esther's assessment that Naomi didn't like Andy.

"He was working very hard to get Eli to delay joining as well," Naomi said. And then Cheryl understood what was underneath Naomi's words. She didn't mind so much if Andy hadn't decided yet on whether to join the church, but she did not like the boy trying to influence her son to stay away. Thankfully, Eli was a member now.

"Well, let's see what he has to say for himself," Cheryl said, and, following Naomi's instructions, she pulled into a long driveway that snaked up a hilly yard. It had been plowed thoroughly, Cheryl was delighted to see. It could be disastrous to go slipping and sliding off this one.

"This is quite a driveway to plow," Cheryl said.

"Oh, they do not plow it themselves," Naomi said, her eyebrows raised. "Four strong sons, but they hire an Englisch snowplow to come through after every snow."

"Oh." Cheryl hadn't realized that was allowed. But now that she thought about it, it didn't seem much different from hiring someone to drive them around, so why not? What surprised her more, though, was Naomi's tone. Cheryl was getting the sense that Naomi's feelings about this family ran deeper than just not approving of Andy's attitude.

Eventually, she crested a small hill and saw a large white house. It was well-proportioned, with a wing off the main entrance in either direction and a graceful look that made it look...well, it didn't look like an Amish farmhouse, she guessed. It had the sort of old-fashioned charm she'd mostly seen among wealthy New Englanders. The yard was covered by a layer of snow, but she could see that it was flat and bordered by a stand of mature trees, and the barn behind the house was large.

"Larry, Joyce's husband, inherited a successful lumber business from his father," Naomi said by way of explanation.

"Ah." Cheryl didn't know what to make of that, but it was clear Naomi was indicating the family had money. Cheryl couldn't help but wonder how much that affected her attitude about Andy.

A few minutes later they knocked on the door, and it was opened by a mousy-looking woman with light brown hair.

"Naomi," she said with a tight smile. She barely glanced at Cheryl, though Cheryl didn't detect any malice in her.

They chatted for a few minutes, and then Naomi asked if they could speak to Andy.

"Ach, I am sorry, he is out at work," she said, though she didn't look all that sorry to Cheryl.

"Do you know when he might be back?" Cheryl asked. "We're anxious to ask him a few questions."

"I would guess this evening, but I do not know for sure," she said.

"Could you let him know that we would like to speak to him?" Naomi asked.

"Of course." The woman's tight smile reappeared. They thanked her, and a moment later they were back in Cheryl's car.

"See?" Naomi said, like she'd proven some great point.

"See what?" Cheryl said, laughing a bit.

"She did not even invite us in."

Cheryl had to admit that hadn't happened very often in the times she'd visited the Amish. Typically she'd been invited in and welcomed as family, not left on the porch.

"And she doesn't know when Andy will be back?" Naomi shook her head, clearly disgusted by this piece of news. It actually didn't seem that strange to Cheryl. Most nineteen-year-olds she knew did not run their plans past their mothers, even if they did still live at home. But Cheryl knew better than to say so. She simply nodded and steered the car toward the Miller farm.

A few minutes later, she said good-bye to Naomi and promised to keep her posted on what she learned. Levi was nowhere in sight, so she was a teeny bit disappointed that she hadn't gotten to see him. He was probably working hard somewhere nearby.

But as she pulled away from the farm, headed back toward the shop, she got an idea.

She made a quick U-turn. This was something she needed to do.

CHAPTER FIVE

The closest hospital to Sugarcreek was in Dover, less than a twenty-minute drive from Main Street. It took a bit longer for Cheryl, since she tried to drive carefully along the slick back country roads. But the highways were clear, and she easily parked and found the main entrance to the big modern building. A friendly woman at the reception desk directed her to room 413 to see Kathy Kimble.

Kathy was watching a daytime talk show on the TV screen above her bed when Cheryl walked in. She turned toward the door, and a big smile crossed her face when Cheryl stepped inside.

"Cheryl! It's so good to see you," Kathy said. She reached for the remote control near her bed and muted the sound.

"Sorry to disturb your viewing," Cheryl said with a smirk.

"Ugh, I had no idea daytime TV was so bad. But I'm bored enough that I would have watched just about anything. Thank you so much for coming." She gestured for Cheryl to sit down in the chair by the bed. "Keith was here all night, but he had to go into work a few hours ago, and I'm bored out of my mind."

"Of course." Kathy was upbeat and her voice was chipper, but she looked pale and drawn. She was wearing a pale blue hospital gown and covered with a thin blanket, and the adjustable bed was positioned so she was leaning back against it. She was hooked up to an IV and some machine that seemed to be monitoring her heart rate.

"How are you doing?" Cheryl asked. She took off her coat and lowered herself down into the chair next to Kathy's bed.

"Much better," Kathy said.

"What happened?" Cheryl asked. The room was small but private, and Kathy had a window that looked out over a stand of trees and her own bathroom. The walls were painted a pukey mauve color, and a washed-out watercolor print of a basket of dried flowers was the only decoration on the walls.

Kathy shook her head, and her hair rubbed against the thin sheet. "I am not even sure, honestly. All I know is that yesterday afternoon I started feeling horrible. I got nauseous, and then I started puking. It came on really quickly, and it didn't really feel like the flu, so I wondered if it was something I ate. Well, then... This is kind of gross... Then I puked again and I noticed blood, so I freaked out a bit."

"As you should," Cheryl said, nodding.

"I've never had that happen before. I called Keith, and he insisted I come straight to the emergency room. I thought he was overreacting, honestly, but when I got here they told me I'd done the right thing, and they gave me all kinds of medicine and set me up with an IV and did all kinds of tests."

"Have they determined what it is?" Cheryl could hear nurses talking and laughing in the hallway.

Kathy grimaced. "They're saying it might be poison in my food. Like, not just food poisoning, but that someone actually put poison into my food. Which is crazy, so I don't..."

"It's not crazy," Cheryl said.

"What?"

"It's not crazy. There actually was poison in your food, as it turns out."

"What?" Kathy's face reflected her confusion. So the news hadn't traveled far yet.

Cheryl explained about Naomi's jam testing positive for rat poison and about some of the jam in her shop being tainted. She told her that at least one other woman, a tourist who had bought the jam at the Swiss Miss, had been hospitalized as well.

"Oh my goodness," Kathy said, her voice shaking. "I can't... Are you sure?"

Cheryl nodded. "I'm afraid so."

"But..." Kathy was at a loss for words. "But how?"

Cheryl explained what they'd uncovered so far and that she was trying to figure out how the poison had ended up in the jam.

"But how is that possible?" Kathy's eyes were wide.

"That's what I'm trying to figure out," Cheryl said. "Let me ask you something. You opened a new jar of jam, right? That's what Heather told me," Cheryl said.

"Yes. Brand-new. It was a jar Naomi had given me for my birthday. I was hungry yesterday afternoon and made myself a turkey and jam sandwich."

It still sounded odd to Cheryl, but she didn't realize she'd grimaced until Kathy laughed.

"Hey, don't knock it until you try it."

"No thanks." Cheryl laughed too. "I'm glad you like it though. But let me ask you a question. When you opened the jar, was it sealed properly?"

Kathy thought for a minute and then nodded. "I am sure it was. I guess I didn't notice specifically, but I know that I would have noticed if it hadn't been sealed. So it must have been."

That was what Cheryl had thought—and what she had been afraid of. That meant the jam had been poisoned before it had been sealed.

"How is the other woman? The tourist?" Kathy asked.

Cheryl admitted that she didn't know, but she knew she needed to find out.

"Wow." Kathy pulled the sheet up and smoothed it out. "I guess I should be grateful I was the only one who ate the jam at my restaurant. Cheryl, you have to get Naomi to go to the police," Kathy said. "This is a criminal activity."

Cheryl knew that Kathy was probably right. She knew it would be a tough sell for her Amish friend though. The Amish were averse to involving the police except in the most extreme matters.

"I know. I will talk to Naomi about it again," she said, though she wasn't optimistic.

They chatted for a few minutes more, and then when a nurse came in to check on Kathy, Cheryl reluctantly said good-bye. She took a moment to pray for her friend, asking the Lord to bless her and heal her completely, and then she said good-bye as a nurse checked her vitals.

"I'll see you soon," Cheryl promised.

"I'll be all caught up on bad television by then." Kathy laughed, and Cheryl walked down the hall feeling lighter than she had when she'd arrived.

She got back into her car and headed toward Sugarcreek. The miles of farmland flew by, and before she knew it, she was driving down Route 39. She checked the time. Esther's shift would end shortly, and she would need to get back to relieve her, but she had time to make one more stop, Cheryl decided. And she'd better do it now because if she let herself, she would put it off indefinitely, and it was something she knew she needed to do.

Cheryl turned off the main road on to a side street and followed it for half a mile until she saw the Village Inn Bed-and-Breakfast. It was a large two-story inn with brick and clapboard siding and a porch that looked warm and inviting, even at this time of year. She stood on the front porch and hesitated. Did she knock? Should she go on in? Finally she settled on ringing the doorbell, and she heard it echo inside the house. A moment later, Molly Bakker opened the door. Molly was a petite woman with dark hair and dark eyes, and her face lit up when she saw Cheryl.

"Cheryl Cooper!" she exclaimed and pulled her into a hug like she was a long-lost friend. "It's good to see you. Come in, come in. Get out of this cold. Isn't this weather terrible?" She closed the door behind Cheryl, who had stepped into a small foyer area at the base of a set of handsome mahogany stairs. The walls in the main hallway were painted a robin's egg blue above a white chair rail, with white bead board beneath. It was a stately and inviting entrance.

"Hi there." Cheryl shifted awkwardly. "I was looking for one of your guests."

"Oh, you mean Ted. He's upstairs, I think. I can check for you if you'd like?"

"I actually don't know his name. He's tall, gray hair?"

"That's my one and only guest. Well, he and his wife Audra, poor thing. But she's still in the hospital. Did you hear about that? She got sick on their vacation, and she's in the hospital. It's just awful. That's the only reason Ted is still here, actually. Of course I am not charging him for the nights he has to stay while Audra is in the hospital."

This all came out in one breath, and Cheryl struggled to keep up. But she smiled when Molly said, "I'll go knock on his door and see if he's available. Would you like to wait in the parlor?" She pointed to a room off to the left.

Cheryl thanked her and stepped into the parlor while Molly went up the stairs. The room was beautiful, with a big bowed window and lush rugs over original hardwood. The walls in here were a rich eggplant color with creamy white accents. The high-backed settee was done in crewelwork, and a glass-front curio cabinet held a collection of beautifully mismatched bone china teacups. A side table was set with a coffee urn and hot water, and a selection of teas and cookies looked tempting.

Cheryl heard footsteps on the stairs, and she braced herself for what she knew would be an uncomfortable meeting. A moment later, Molly stepped into the room, followed by the man who'd left her shop in a huff just yesterday.

He nodded when he saw her. "What do you want?"

Cheryl took a deep breath. Her natural instinct was to fight; sucking up her pride did not come easily. "I came to apologize."

That answer seemed to knock him completely off balance. A bit of the anger went out of his face, replaced by wariness. Cheryl continued quickly, before she had the nerve to change her mind.

"I'm sorry that I wasn't more understanding when you came in yesterday. It turns out you were right. The jam is what made your wife sick."

He nodded without saying a word. Molly, who was hovering in the doorway, let out a small gasp.

"We had the jam tested, and it turns out rat poison was added to it. Obviously I didn't know that when I sold the jam, but I am so glad your wife got medical attention right away. And I wanted to know how she's doing."

It took him a minute to answer. He seemed to be struggling with how to respond.

But then he spoke, and his words chilled her.

"Rat poison?" he said, shaking his head. "You sold my wife jam laced with *rat poison*?"

"I'm sorry I..." Cheryl struggled for words that would defuse the situation, but he was just getting started.

"I am missing work and stuck in this backwater town while my wife struggles for her life because you sold her poisoned jam?" His cheeks were turning a deep shade of pink. "Do you have any idea how much this is costing us, between medical bills and staying here and missing work? Not to mention the intangibles like pain and suffering? Not just for us, but for the whole family? Our son can't even focus on his college classes, and our daughter was ready to drop everything and come be by her mother's side," he said, his voice rising with each word.

"Like I said, I am sorry about…"

"You're sorry. I got it. And I guess you think that is going to make up for everything?" His fists were balled up at his side. "Well, your sorry isn't going to prevent a lawsuit, if that's what you're thinking. My brother is a lawyer, and…"

"I don't think that's what she was trying to say," Molly said, jumping into the fray. Cheryl shot her a grateful look. "I think Cheryl was genuinely trying to apologize for her mistake and wanted to see how Audra was doing. That's all." There was a note of authority in her voice that took even the man by surprise.

"Well," he said. He took in a deep breath that puffed up his chest. "Be that as it may, I just want to make it clear that this is not over. You can expect to hear from my lawyer when I get back to Columbus."

Cheryl didn't know how to respond. A thousand things flew through her mind, none of which would sound very Christian. Instead of answering right away, she tried to focus her mind on the verse in Ephesians 4:29, which her pastor had preached on Sunday: "Do not let any unwholesome talk come out of your mouths, but only what is helpful for building others up according to their needs, that it may benefit those who listen." It was the last thing Cheryl wanted to do, but she knew it was the right thing to do. She also thought about how Naomi would respond in a situation like this and tried to channel Naomi's calm, sure demeanor.

"I pray that will not be necessary. Please feel free to contact me if you need anything more," Cheryl said and pulled a business card from her wallet. She handed it to the man, and then before he could say anything more—or before she could—she turned and walked out the door.

She made it to her car before she started crying. Then the tears fell freely. How could he... She came here to... She couldn't believe how *nasty* he had been. She dug a tissue out of the pack in her purse and swiped at her eyes, and she blew her nose. She sat for a minute, trying to compose herself before she set out on the road, but thoughts kept pinging around in her brain.

Well, she wasn't sure what would happen next, but a few things became clear as she sat there and thought through this. She knew that Naomi did not want to report the matter to the police, but if the man was talking about suing, they needed to report the matter. Naomi needed it to be on record that someone had tampered with her jam. If he sued, she could lose everything—the farm, the house, the petting zoo—if they couldn't prove she hadn't done it. And Cheryl was liable as well. If he sued the Swiss Miss, Aunt Mitzi could lose everything, and she might even have to come home from Papua New Guinea. Cheryl couldn't let that happen.

They needed to figure out who had poisoned that jam right away.

Chapter Six

Cheryl stepped inside the Sugarcreek Police department a few minutes later. She had called the shop and asked if Esther could stay a little later, and she had been fine with that since Jessica Stockton wasn't coming to give her a ride home until four anyway. The brick building had white gingerbread trim on the roof and a large picture window with decorative shutters, and Cheryl believed it had to be the most charming police station in Ohio.

Once inside, she waved to Delores Delgado, who was sitting at the counter that divided the waiting area from the offices at the back. Cheryl explained that she was here to see Chief Twitchell, and Delores called his office. The police chief invited her to send Cheryl in. Cheryl thanked her, and then she opened the frosted glass door that led to the back of the station. She waved to Officer Anderson, who was hunched over a desk staring at a computer screen, and she made her way to the familiar office of the Sugarcreek Police Chief.

"Hello, Cheryl," he said. He was in his midforties and had salt-and-pepper hair and a Southern drawl that marked him as not from around here. He gestured for her to sit down in one of the green vinyl chairs that sat opposite his desk. "What can I do for you today?"

"I'd like to report a crime," Cheryl said. "Someone put poison in Naomi Miller's strawberry jam."

A smile crossed his face, but he quickly suppressed it and tried to compose his face.

"I'm sorry. I must not be understandin' this correctly. You want the police to investigate jam?"

"It's not just jam," Cheryl said. "It's that someone put rat poison in the jam. And people are getting sick from it. But Naomi didn't do it, and I'm trying to figure out who did."

"Are you sure about this?" he said, raising an eyebrow. "I can see that you're upset, but I guess I'm not seein' what you want the police to do about the fact that people have been gettin' sick from some jam."

"It's not just that people have been getting sick from some jam," Cheryl said, her frustration rising. "Someone— someone other than Naomi—put rat poison into her jam. And Kathy Kimble is in the hospital because of it. And there's a tourist in town who also got sick from it, and her husband is threatening to sue."

Chief Twitchell eyed her. "And you're sure this jam has been tampered with? How do you know it's rat poison?" He took a breath, and then he spoke slowly and carefully, as if explaining something to a toddler. "Is there any chance the jam might have simply gone bad?"

Cheryl quickly explained what she knew and that she had a list of people she'd been looking into, and he dutifully took a report, but Cheryl could see by the look on his face that he wasn't taking this seriously.

Well, it may be just some mix-up involving jam that had gone bad to him, but at least official record has been made, she thought as she exited the police station and headed back toward the Swiss Miss.

One thing was clear to her though: she shouldn't expect the police to jump all over this case. Judging by his reaction, if she wanted to find out who had poisoned Naomi's jam, she was going to have to do it herself.

When Cheryl got back to the shop, Esther had everything under control, just like Cheryl knew she would. She said the traffic had been slow, but Cheryl had expected that for a wintry Tuesday afternoon. She had managed to sell a set of quilted place mats, a set of hand-carved salad forks, and a pound of bulk candy, so it wasn't a complete waste of time. And the shelves were tidy and well-stocked, except for the gaping hole where the jam had been, and the shop warm and cheerful. Cheryl thanked her, and Esther set off. Cheryl was glad she was getting a ride home on a day like today, when her bike could be treacherous.

Cheryl looked around the shop. There wasn't really anything to do out here, and there were no customers. There was still an hour before she typically closed up. Cheryl should probably use the time to catch up on e-mails and invoices and work on payroll, but she couldn't stop thinking about the jam, and about Andy, and Martha, and whether either of them could have been the one to put poison into the jam.

There was still one person she hadn't looked into yet, and it was probably her best bet, in some ways. She pulled a phone book from the shelf behind the counter and tried to figure out where to look. Freezer repair? She started with the *F*s. She looked through the section but didn't find the right ad, so she flipped to *A* and looked through Appliance Repair.

And there she found an ad for Alamo Appliance Repair. The ad said the employees were trained to fix both electric and propane-powered appliances. And the ad had a star in it. This had to be the company that Naomi called the day her freezer went out. Cheryl located the number and picked up the store phone. She dialed the number, and it rang and rang. Finally, voice mail picked up, and Cheryl left a message asking for someone to call her back.

The shop was still empty. It had been dead all day. She looked down at the pile of invoices she still needed to work on but decided that they could wait. She might as well close up for the day.

Cheryl closed out the cash register and straightened up the store, sweeping and taking out the trash. Just as she was about to turn off the lights, the phone rang. Cheryl dived for it, thinking it was the appliance repairman calling her back.

"Hello?" Cheryl asked breathlessly.

"Hi, Cheryl. It is Naomi."

"Naomi?" Cheryl could hear the wind whistling in the background. She must be calling from the phone shanty in her backyard. Which must mean she had stomped through ankle-deep snow and was shivering in the bitter cold even now. Which must mean that whatever she had called to say was important.

"I just heard from Greta Yoder," Naomi said. "Two people who ate at her restaurant this morning, before we told her about the jam, have been taken to the hospital."

CHAPTER SEVEN

Cheryl hurried over to Yoder's Corner and asked for Greta Yoder at the front. The young Amish girl at the hostess stand asked her to wait, and she returned a few moments later with Greta, who ushered Cheryl into the restaurant. The restaurant was not very crowded, as it was still a bit early for dinner, and Greta and Cheryl sat down at one of the big round dining tables.

Yoder's Corner was run by Greta and her husband August, who did most of the cooking. The place served good old-fashioned down-home cooking, and their specialties were homemade sausages and cinnamon rolls as big as plates. The food was delicious, and it also explained why both Greta and August carried a few extra pounds.

"I'm sorry to bother you," Cheryl said. "I know you must be getting ready to serve dinner." Amish girls in long dresses were laying out silverware and carrying pitchers of water, preparing for the dinner rush.

"I am glad you came." Greta's face, usually warm and full of life, looked pained. "I am heartbroken about the two people who got sick from eating at our restaurant."

"Well, they got sick from the jam, which is not something you and August made," Cheryl said, trying to be kind.

"It does not matter," Greta said. "I just wish... I did not know..."

"I wish we had been able to let you know sooner," Cheryl said gently. "You serve Naomi's jam all the time, don't you?"

Greta nodded. "That is right. I have served it for years. Whenever someone orders toast, we serve it with a bit of jam in a little dish."

Cheryl nodded. She'd seen that before.

"Did you recently get a new shipment from Naomi?"

"Yes." Greta nodded. "Just a few days back. Her strawberry jam is so popular that I told her we needed more. The jam we have been serving is from Naomi's latest batch."

So it was from the same batch Cheryl had been selling in her shop then. The batch made that fateful day. Which meant that it was nearly certain these two diners had gotten sick from the jam, not something else.

"Do you have any idea how many people were served jam in the past few days?"

Greta blew out a breath. "I do not know. Dozens, probably."

"But only two have gotten sick?"

"Only two that I know of."

Cheryl thought two wasn't too bad, really. Well, it was two more than they wanted, obviously, but considering how many people might have been affected, they were lucky it was just two so far.

"Do you know anything about them?"

"One was a customer. An Englisch man who ate here this morning for breakfast. He has eaten here a few times, though I do not know much about him. I believe he is a salesman of some sort. The other is Leigha, one of my servers."

"She ate jam this morning too?"

"Yes. The girls work hard for long hours, and they are welcome to eat the food we serve on their breaks. She had toast with jam during her midmorning break."

"How did you find out they had been taken to the hospital?"

"Leigha's mother, Susannah, called me a little while ago to tell me she was vomiting up blood and they were taking her to the hospital. Leigha mentioned that something had tasted a bit off in the jam she ate here, and she wondered if that was what caused it."

Interesting. This was the first time someone had mentioned they'd tasted the poison.

"Off how?"

"She said it was too sweet, almost like Kool-Aid."

"But she kept eating it?"

Greta shrugged. "She is young."

Cheryl couldn't fault her. It must not have tasted that strange, since no one else had even noticed an off flavor yet.

"Anyway, when she was in the emergency room at the hospital, the doctors mentioned that another man had just come in with the same symptoms. She caught a glimpse of him as they wheeled him into an exam room, and she recognized him as the man she had served this morning."

"Oh, goodness. I am so sorry, Greta. Do you know how they're doing?"

"Leigha's mother told me she was doing okay. They had gotten her some medicines, and it seemed that she was going to be fine."

"I sure hope that's true."

Greta nodded. "I am just thankful you and Naomi told me about the jam so I did not continue serving it. I can only hope that no one else ate any before I pulled the jars."

Cheryl hoped so as well.

"Have you found out how the poison got into the jam yet?" Greta asked. "You are looking into it, yes?"

"Yes." Cheryl nodded. "I certainly am. And I have some suspicions, but nothing solid yet. And the police are looking into it as well."

"That is good," Greta said. "I am glad about that."

Cheryl was too. Now it was not just Naomi and the Swiss Miss that were liable. The Amish were nonlitigious by nature, so she didn't worry that Leigha's family would sue Greta and August, but the English salesman might not see things that way, especially if he had high medical bills to cover as a result.

"I will do everything I can to figure out who did this," Cheryl promised. "And please keep me posted if you hear of any more customers who get sick."

"I will." Greta pushed herself up. "Thank you, Cheryl."

Cheryl headed home with a heavy heart. Now there were four people who'd been sickened by the jam and probably more to come. She needed to find answers. Quickly.

After Cheryl went home and ate dinner, she decided to go down to the basement where she'd stashed a bunch of her things when she'd moved to Aunt Mitzi's house. She flipped on the light at the top of the stairs, and the wooden steps creaked as she went down. Cheryl hadn't spent much time in the basement since she'd lived here. Basements were dank and dark and they all smelled funny, and this one was no exception. But, she had to admit as she stepped out on to the concrete floor, this one was at least warm, and all the scary infrastructure like the hot water heater and the boiler were tucked away in a closet at the far end.

She looked around. Along one wall were dozens of clear plastic storage bins that held Aunt Mitzi's things she hadn't taken with her. Each was neatly labeled, so if she ever needed Cheryl to send her a wool sweater or a specific Christmas decoration or her scrapbooking supplies, Cheryl would know exactly where to look.

Against the opposite wall were cardboard boxes, piled here and there, that contained Cheryl's things. They were not labeled, and scattered among them were also a few pieces of good antique furniture she couldn't part with but didn't need in this furnished house, a guitar she hadn't played in years, and, somewhere in there, skis.

Cheryl moved aside a cardboard box and then another, looking for the long fiberglass skis. How hard could it be to find them? They didn't exactly blend in with the boxes. After moving several boxes aside, Cheryl finally found them lying on the floor against the wall. There were two pairs of skis, as well as poles and boots. She picked up the set that was on top.

They were pink and white, and they were dinged and well-worn, but as Cheryl examined them now, memories flooded her mind. Her parents had given her these skis for her fourteenth birthday, and she had used them on many happy weekend excursions and day trips with her family. She had so many good memories of those early ski trips with her family. True, they were hardly tackling the Alps. Nor were their ski trips the luxurious spa weekends people thought about these days. If the Coopers stayed overnight near the mountains, it was at some budget motel where they ate food Cheryl's mother—a defiant nonskier—had packed for them ahead of time. Her father was a pastor, after all, not some celebrity who traveled the world in search of hot spots. But her father had seen those trips as family time, and Cheryl had relished them. Those had been wonderful days, zooming down the mountain with her dad and brother, laughing and spending evenings together. She'd been so excited when she had received this pair of skis, not just because it meant an end to renting subpar equipment at the mountain, but also because it meant more long weekends with her father.

She set that pair aside and looked over the newer, sleeker pair underneath. They were black and neon yellow, and the bindings were high quality. These were top-of-the-line skis, designed for speed. She had worn them maybe twice, and they still looked brand-new.

These, she thought, running her hands over the smooth fiberglass, had been a gift from her ex-fiancé Lance. She knew they were supremely expensive, and that was part of what made them a good gift in his eyes. Cheryl remembered when she'd unwrapped them, her first reaction was that she wished he'd put the money toward a ring instead. Still, they'd had a nice time skiing on them, and Cheryl was grateful for them now. Two pairs of skis meant she could teach both Eli and Levi the basics at the same time, as long as they could fit into her boots. Both pairs were adjustable, so she hoped they might work.

She hauled both sets of skis upstairs, along with the accompanying poles and bindings, and set them by the door. She didn't have a roof rack, so she would have to figure out how to maneuver them to fit mostly inside the car, no doubt sticking out through an open window, but she would do that tomorrow. She peeked out the front window. It had stopped snowing, but the sky was still covered in a layer of clouds, and she could see from the streetlights that the ground was covered in a fine powder, like superfine sugar. She opened the door and tossed some rock salt on to the front path, but it wasn't enough to be worth shoveling.

For now, she closed the door and thought about how she'd approach ski lessons for two Amish men who'd never worn skis in their lives. She'd start with the snowplow, probably, and...

But as she looked out at the snow, her mind drifted back to Aunt Mitzi and to her missing snow. There was plenty of it here. If only there was some way to ship some of it to her. It wasn't possible...was it?

Cheryl turned away from the window and grabbed her laptop and sat down on the couch. Beau jumped up beside her and started kneading her leg with his paw. She gently moved him, and he settled down next to her, resting against her leg. How would you even go about trying to ship snow to the other side of the world? It was a crazy idea, but Cheryl imagined her aunt's face as she opened a box of fluffy white powder from back home, and she decided it was at least worth investigating.

Cheryl did an Internet search for "shipping snow" and was delighted to see that there were actually services out there designed to do just that. One company in Boston promised to ship good, old New England snow anywhere in the country. They used Styrofoam containers and ice packs and shipped large boxes overnight via FedEx. It was a funny idea, and she wondered if maybe they could ship to Aunt Mitzi, but—whoa. Was that the price? Cheryl thought she must have added a digit in her mind. But no, she looked again, and the price remained the same. Crazy expensive. And that was just to ship within the United States.

Beau nuzzled her hand, and she petted him absently.

Well, maybe she didn't need to use some fancy service to ship snow. She had plenty of snow right here. She could get a Styrofoam box and some ice packs.... She went to the Web site of the international shipping company that delivered packages to Aunt Mitzi in Papua New Guinea. She used a calculator tool on their site to see how much it might cost to ship a box the quickest way possible. *Let's see...* Well, it looked like the fastest available method would still take several weeks to reach Aunt Mitzi. That wouldn't work very well. And how much did snow weigh? She thought about it for a minute and realized that a light and fluffy snowflake might seem almost weightless, but combined with other snowflakes, they sure would add up. Shoveling a walkway was a workout because snow was actually quite heavy. And she would need a lot of it to keep the temperature low enough to prevent the snow from all melting. So, say the package weighed twenty pounds, and if she shipped it the fastest way...

Cheryl's eyes widened at the number on the screen.

Okay, so that wouldn't work then. She wasn't going to spend several hundred dollars to send a package that would most likely end up at Aunt Mitzi's as water anyway.

Well, so shipping actual snow to Aunt Mitzi probably wouldn't work. But Cheryl was determined to think of some way to let her aunt know she was thinking of her, and to remind her of the joys—ha!—of winter.

CHAPTER EIGHT

Wednesday morning started out unexpectedly busy at the Swiss Miss. The sky had cleared, and though the temperature was still frigid, the better weather and clear roads seemed to have brought people out of hibernation. Cheryl sold through her stock of handmade soap, and a tour group from Indiana bought out most of the wooden toys, even a snow globe. It was too bad she didn't have Naomi's jam to sell because she was certain it would have flown off the shelves. Fortunately, Lydia Troyer was working a shift this morning, and she was able to help ring up customers quickly and efficiently, and the women in the tour group seemed delighted to meet a real Amish girl.

Finally, the crowds cleared out for the most part, and while Lydia used the lull to restock the shelves, Cheryl decided to do a bit more research. She still hadn't gotten a call back from Alamo Appliance Repair, so she called them again. When no one picked up, she turned to her computer. She pulled up a browser window, typed in the name of the company, and hit Return.

Several listings popped up. Cheryl clicked on the first and saw that it was a very basic Web site with the company's information. There was just one landing page, and all it contained was the name of the company and address and phone number, as well as a few quotes from satisfied customers. The company was based in New Philadelphia, she saw. But still that wasn't very helpful.

Cheryl clicked back to the search page and came across what looked like a site where people could review businesses. She clicked on that page, and a handful of reviews of Alamo Appliance Repair came up. Cheryl read through them and discovered that people seemed generally pleased with the service they'd gotten. She also read that it was a family business and that several people did repairs. Two were mentioned in the reviews, a Stan and a Nick. Could either one of them be the person who had been in Naomi's basement the day the jam had been poisoned? Cheryl looked around the shop. It was quiet now, and Lydia was here. No one at the repair company was answering the phone. She didn't know which one of the repairmen had been in Naomi's house that day, but Cheryl could think of only one way to find out.

"Lydia?" Cheryl called, pulling off her apron. "I'm going to go out for a bit."

"Have fun," Lydia called.

Cheryl wasn't sure fun was on the agenda, but she hoped she would find some answers. She pulled on her coat and her hat, grabbed her purse, and headed out to her car. Once she had the engine on and the heater running, she used her phone to look up the address listed in the ad and quickly found the quickest route. It would only take about twenty minutes to get there.

Cheryl set off, and as she drove, her mind wandered, thinking through what she knew so far about the suspects. None of them wanted to believe that poor little Martha could have made a mistake of this magnitude, but it was a possibility. She needed to talk to Andy, Eli's friend who had been there the day they made jam. Or maybe she wouldn't. Hopefully she would find the answer here, at Alamo Appliance Repairs.

But what if none of these were the right answer? Was there something she was missing? Some possibility she hadn't thought of? Cheryl's mind conjured images of rival jam makers trying to sabotage Naomi's successful business and serial killers out to poison large groups of people anonymously. None of them seemed likely.

Cheryl hadn't figured out any more likely scenarios by the time she pulled up in front of the address listed in the ad. It turned out to be a two-story white house in a residential neighborhood. She had never been to this part of town, and the houses on the street had seen better days, with cracked sidewalks and peeling paint and abandoned cars on several of the lawns. But Cheryl was pleased to see that in front of the house her GPS led her to, there was a van with Alamo Appliance Repair painted on the side. At least she knew she'd found the right place.

Cheryl climbed out and went up to the door cautiously. Iron posts, painted white, flanked the small concrete front step. She knocked on the door, and a few moments later an older man in baggy jeans and a white undershirt answered the door. Suspenders kept the jeans up over his round belly.

"Hi. I'm looking for Alamo Appliance Repair," Cheryl said, trying to make herself look nonthreatening. She got the sense that they didn't get too many customers coming here.

"Yeah?" the man said, eyeing her. He hadn't shaved in a few days, and his beard was coming in gray.

"Someone from your company repaired a freezer for a friend of mine last month, and she's hoping to get in touch with him," Cheryl said, smiling way too brightly.

"Something wrong with the work we did?"

Cheryl could hear the sound of a television playing inside the house.

"No, nothing like that. She's quite pleased with the work, in fact. The freezer works perfectly now."

"But she wants to talk to the man?" He narrowed his eyes, and something seemed to register for him. "You the one that called here yesterday?"

"Yes, that was me," Cheryl said. "My friend is anxious to speak to the person who came to her house." She didn't elaborate. If she tried to explain why she wanted to talk to the repairman, he'd never tell her anything. "But she wasn't sure of the man's name, so I told her I'd try to find out for her."

"Why didn't your friend come here herself to ask?" The man wasn't unfriendly, exactly. It was more like he didn't know what to make of her.

"She's Amish," Cheryl said. "Getting here in her buggy would have taken quite a long time."

"Ah. If she's Amish, it was Stan who repaired her freezer. He's the one who does all the propane appliances."

"Stan?"

"McCullough. My son."

"Wonderful." Cheryl had a name at least. "Is he here by any chance? I'd really love to speak with him."

"Nah. He's at his place. I call him when there's a job for him."

"Oh." He didn't live here then. "Is there any way you could tell me where that is?"

The man eyed her uncertainly. He hitched up his pants. "Tell you what. I can give you his phone number. From there it's up to him."

"That would be so helpful."

"You got a pen?"

Cheryl pulled out her phone and held it up. "I'll put it here."

That seemed to make him even more suspicious, but he rattled off a number, and Cheryl put it into her phone and labeled it Stan the Repairman.

"Thanks so much for your help," Cheryl said, again just a shade too brightly.

The man grunted, and then he stepped back and closed the door. Customer service at its best. Still, she had gotten what she came for, she supposed, or at least a step in the right direction.

She didn't want to call Stan from her car while it was still parked in front of the house, so she drove to the shopping center at the end of the street and parked in front of a Kmart and placed the call.

The phone rang and rang, and finally she was dumped into the voice mail for Stan McCullough. She left a message, asking to speak to him at his convenience.

Then she turned around and drove back to Sugarcreek. Lydia was ringing up a woman who was buying out the stock of quilted pot holders. Esther had come in for her shift and was there as well, dusting and straightening. Cheryl said hello to both of them and chatted with the woman for a few minutes before she left.

"How were things here?" Cheryl asked.

"Just fine. No problems," Lydia said. "Did you have any luck?"

"Maybe," Cheryl said. "It's hard to tell."

"I certainly hope you find the person who did this soon. Maam was so worried she hardly slept at all last night," Esther said.

"I hope I do too," Cheryl said. She looked around the store and eyed the computer. Now that she had a full name, she was interested to see what she could find out about this repairman. "In fact, if you guys have things covered here, I'll do a bit of research."

"Of course," Lydia said, and she grabbed a rag and went around the counter to begin dusting. The two Amish girls chattered in their language. Cheryl understood just enough to realize they were talking about the upcoming Singing that seemed to have all the youth in a tizzy. She smiled and turned to the store's computer, shaking the mouse to wake it up.

She typed the name Stan McCullough into the browser and hit Return.

The first thing that came up was a social media site. She clicked on his profile and scanned the posts and pictures. From what she could tell, he seemed to be in his midthirties, a die-hard Buckeyes fan, and very involved with fantasy football. He had graduated from a high school in New Philadelphia, but there was no college listed. Most of the pictures he posted were of his dog or comments on the weather. She scanned the page, looking for anything that might have been a clue as to whether he was behind the poisoning, but nothing jumped out.

She went back to the search page and saw listings for LinkedIn profiles, White Pages, and other fairly useless pages. Then something at the bottom of the screen caught her eye. An article in the Canton *Repository* where his name came up. She clicked on the link, and when she saw the headline, her mouth fell open.

It couldn't be...

CHAPTER NINE

Cheryl looked at the newspaper article on her screen, the one that had come up when she'd searched for Stan McCullough. The headline read Trucker Convicted of Poisoning; Will Face Jail Time.

Well now. Cheryl enlarged the article and read it quickly, then went back and read it carefully to make sure she'd understood. It seemed that Stan McCullough hadn't always been in appliance repair. Before he'd joined the family business, he had been a long-haul trucker, and he'd been married. He'd become convinced that his wife was having an affair with a fellow trucker while he was out on the road. Apparently, he'd decided the best way to take care of that would be to get rid of the man, and he'd been arrested for lacing the man's coffee with antifreeze while they'd both been at the café at the same truck stop. The man, identified as Dean Schmidt, had been taken to a local hospital and ended up fine, but Stan had been arrested—and convicted—of trying to poison his rival.

He'd put antifreeze in the man's coffee? Cheryl shook her head. How did that even work? Had he been carrying around a jug of antifreeze when he went into the café? Wasn't antifreeze fluorescent green? Didn't that stand out, even in a cup of coffee? And how did the man not notice a noxious chemical in his coffee and drink it?

Cheryl opened up anther browser window and did a search for "antifreeze in coffee." It didn't take long to find several relevant articles online that addressed this very topic. Apparently, this was far more common, at least in online chatter, than she'd realized. And she quickly discovered that antifreeze—or, more specifically, the chemical compound ethylene glycol that was the main ingredient in antifreeze—was colorless and flavorless and also had a naturally sweet flavor. It had been used to lace the coffee or tea of unsuspecting victims many times through the years.

Well, she may not ever understand how someone could knowingly put poison in someone else's coffee, but it didn't take a genius to see the connection to Naomi's case. Stan McCullough had been convicted of poisoning a man in the past. It wasn't a bit hard to fathom that he might have done it once again.

Cheryl pulled out her cell phone and tried his number again, but it went straight to voice mail. She'd find a way to get in touch with him though. Now she was even more certain he was behind things.

She turned away from her computer and started to push herself up, but she stopped when she noticed a figure walking toward her. Chief Twitchell. He was headed up the main aisle of the store, his eyes cast down. Lydia and Esther had stopped chattering and were watching silently as he walked.

"Hello, Chief Twitchell," she said when he got to the counter. Her mind raced. What had happened? It must be something bad if he had come to talk to her. What if it was...? Were the two people who had gotten sick yesterday...?

"Mornin', Cheryl." He pulled off his hat and ran a hand through his salt-and-pepper hair to straighten it.

"Did something happen?" She knew she shouldn't assume the worst, but...

"You could say that." He set his hat down on the counter and sighed. "We got a visit from the Honorable Ted Gillingham this morning."

Cheryl searched through the recesses of her mind, but the name didn't ring a bell.

"He's been in the state senate for decades. He and his wife came to Sugarcreek for a little weekend getaway."

Cheryl waited for him to go on.

"He tells me his wife ate some bad jam," he said simply.

"Oh." Cheryl's eyes widened. It was the angry tourist! He was a state senator? What did that even mean? And why had he contacted the police? "Why did...?"

"He wants me to arrest the woman who poisoned his wife," he said simply. "He said, 'She needs to be stopped.'"

Cheryl's first reaction was to laugh. He was here to arrest her? But then her blood ran cold. He wasn't really here to arrest her, was he?

"Needs to be stopped?" Cheryl echoed faintly.

Chief Twitchell nodded. "He says he's plannin' to sue, but after he read today's paper, he realized he needed to 'put an end to this.'"

"Today's paper?"

"You didn't see it?" he asked.

Cheryl shook her head.

"Take a look when you get a chance. In the meantime, I'm not going to arrest Naomi, but..."

"Naomi?" Cheryl interrupted. Not her? She heard Esther gasp from the side of the store. So the Amish girls were listening in.

"Yes, Naomi." He dipped his head. "She's the one who made the 'poisoned' jam, right?"

"Yes, but..."

"Well, then she's the one I should be going after."

"But..."

"But I'm *not*," he said.

Cheryl glanced at Esther and saw that she had relaxed a bit with that news.

"I'm not goin' to arrest Naomi because I can no more imagine her tryin' to poison people with her jam than I can imagine her runnin' for president. But I wanted you to know that I am lookin' into this whole mess now."

Cheryl took a minute to process what he'd said. He wasn't going to arrest Naomi. He was looking into who poisoned the jam. He was suddenly taking the whole thing seriously now that a powerful man had come along asking for answers.

"So you're investigating who put the poison in the jam after all?" she asked.

He let out a long sigh. "Yes, I am."

Cheryl tried not to gloat. This wasn't about being right; it was about making sure no one else got sick. It was about proving

Naomi innocent. And about finding who had poisoned the jam, so Cheryl wouldn't have to face a lawsuit.

"Well, in that case, would you like to hear what I've learned?" she said, brightening.

"No thank you." He shook his head. "My team will be runnin' its own investigation into the matter. That's why I'm here. I need you to tell me about the jam you sold. And to remind you that you need to stay clear of this police investigation," he said, leveling his gaze at her.

Cheryl spent the next few minutes running through the whole thing with him—how often she typically restocked jam, when this latest batch had come in, when she'd sold the one the senator's wife had bought. She gave him the jar of jam, which he used plastic gloves to slip into an evidence bag. He made notes in a small notebook as she talked. He was on his way out to the Miller farm to talk to Naomi next, he said, and then he thanked her and headed out.

Cheryl immediately picked up the phone to try to warn Naomi that the police chief was on his way, but the phone rang and rang and then went to the answering machine. Once again, there was no one in the yard to hear it.

Esther and Lydia were chattering together in Pennsylvania Dutch again as they dusted and straightened the shelves. Well, Esther had obviously heard that the police chief was not about to arrest her mother, but she no doubt had to be frightened by the encounter. Cheryl would talk with Esther in a bit, remind her that there was no danger to her mother, but for now she was glad Lydia was there to talk with her.

Cheryl tried to focus on the things that needed to be done around the shop, but now she was antsy. She tried calling Stan McCullough again, but when he didn't pick up, she didn't leave a message. She tried searching for an address for him, but the phone book didn't have a landline for him, and she couldn't find an address registered to his cell phone anywhere online.

She sat back on the stool and tapped her fingers on the counter. She still needed to talk to Andy, Eli's friend. How could she do that? Then she remembered that she knew where he lived. She popped up.

"I'm going to run out for a bit," Cheryl said. Both girls nodded and then turned back to their conversation.

The first thing she did was run to the Sugarcreek Old Amish Store to pick up a copy of the local daily *Times-Reporter* newspaper. Cheryl was shocked to see a story in the local news section about how four people had been sent to the hospital from eating poisoned jam. The headline was In a Jam. Amish-made Jam Lands Four in Hospital. The story was not at all balanced, but the facts, she had to admit, were correct. She supposed she should be thankful her store had not been named, nor had Yoder's Corner. Still, this could not be good. She was even more determined to find answers now.

But her trip to Andy's house was unfruitful. A teenage girl Cheryl assumed must be one of his sisters answered the door and said he wasn't home. She promised to pass along Cheryl's phone number and ask him to call, but even after Cheryl insisted she was a friend of Naomi's, the girl still looked suspicious.

Cheryl returned to the shop and sent the girls home. And then when it was time to close up the shop, she locked up with a heavy heart. She was no closer to finding out who was behind the poison than she had been this morning.

Would she ever get to the bottom of this?

CHAPTER TEN

After she locked up the Swiss Miss, Cheryl went back to her house and loaded the skis into her car. It took some positioning, and the back window behind her had to be open, but she got the skis to fit. Then she drove, carefully and slowly, to the Millers' house. As she drove, she thought about ski resorts she'd been to. They typically had snow all winter, even if there hadn't been much snow yet in the season. If nature didn't provide the snow they needed, they simply made their own. Was there a way to make snow for Aunt Mitzi? Cheryl would have to look into it, she thought, as she pulled into the Millers' driveway. She parked and pulled the skis out of her car and leaned them against the house.

Naomi and the girls were finishing cleaning up dinner when Elizabeth welcomed Cheryl inside. Naomi ushered her in, carrying the two sets of ski boots under her arm, and Cheryl explained that she had brought her skis. Naomi helped her set the boots down and insisted she sit at the table with a cup of herbal tea while the men finished their chores in the barn, and then she sat down beside her.

"The police came here today," Naomi said as tiny wisps of steam rose from her cup.

"How did it go?"

"It was fine," Naomi said. "I guess I am glad they are trying to find whoever did this. But it is still quite a shock when the police show up at your door."

"They were not as bad as when the reporter came," Esther said, looking up from the sink. She was elbow-deep in soapy water.

"A reporter came here?" Cheryl's mouth fell open. This was not good.

"Yes. He was quite pushy and wanted me to tell him how poison had gotten into my jam. He would not leave until I gave him something to print in his paper."

"What did you tell him?" Cheryl asked. Oh dear. She knew how pushy reporters could sometimes be when they were trying to get a story. She certainly hoped this man had not pushed Naomi into saying something she shouldn't have.

"I gave him a quote," Naomi said, a twinkle in her eye. "I gave it to him in Pennsylvania Dutch."

Cheryl had to laugh. Good for Naomi.

"I'm afraid I'm still not any closer to finding out who is responsible," Cheryl said, and she updated Naomi on what she'd done that day, how she had Stan McCullough's cell phone number, and how she'd tried to talk to Andy again.

"We must ask Eli if Andy has a cell phone," Naomi said. Cheryl nodded. If he hadn't joined the church yet, chances were good he did have one.

Soon the men came back from the barn. Seth came in, nodded at Cheryl, and disappeared up the stairs.

"Did I see what I thought I saw outside?" Eli asked, stomping to get the snow off his boots before he stepped inside.

"I brought my skis."

Eli made a noise that was somewhere between a yelp and a yay, and he turned and gave a high five to Levi, who was standing just behind him. "Let us go now," he said.

Cheryl glanced at Naomi, who gestured that it was fine with her, so Cheryl stood up.

"I will get the skis," Eli called and disappeared out the back door once again.

"Wait," Cheryl called. "Let's make sure these boots fit first."

Cheryl told them to sit at the table, and then she retrieved the boots.

"Levi can take those," Eli said, looking at the pink-and-white boots. He gestured at the sleek black pair. "I will use that pair."

Levi met Cheryl's eye and shrugged. "It does not matter to me."

Cheryl started with Eli, who looked like he was about ready to launch out the back door. She adjusted the black boots to their largest setting, and Eli was able to slip his foot in. She was aware that the whole family was watching them. She showed him how to pull the plastic strap to tighten it, and he stood up and took a few steps in the boots.

"Easy enough so far," he said.

"It will get harder once you add the skis," Cheryl promised.

"I will go get them," Eli said, and when Cheryl nodded, he disappeared out the back door. Then she turned to Levi, who was waiting patiently, eyeing the pink boots nervously.

"I do not think they will fit," he said.

"We'll try to make them," Cheryl said and adjusted them as big as they would go. She carefully helped him slip his feet in. "How does that feel?"

"A bit tight," he said, pushing himself up. "But I think it will work." She helped him tighten the lacing.

Cheryl pulled her hat and coat back on and stepped out the back door. Huh. She hadn't really thought about the fact that it would be dark out, and on an Amish farm, there were no electric lights to brighten the yard. Still, Levi had placed a kerosene lantern on a wooden bench under the roof overhang and another on a snow-covered picnic table, so there was some light, and the cloudless sky allowed a nearly full moon to cover the fields with its milky light.

Plus, she didn't think there would be that much actual skiing tonight, more just explaining how things worked, so she decided it was worth at least giving it a shot. By the time Eli had come around the house, one set of skis and poles under each arm, Levi had brushed the snow off the picnic table and was seated, looking up at her. She tried not to stare at how handsome he looked, the way the moonlight played over the planes of his face.

"I have your pink skis," Eli said, holding them out to Levi.

"I do not mind," Levi said, reaching out to take the skis. "I do not need fancy equipment to beat you at this."

Cheryl recognized this as the Amish version of trash talk, and she laughed.

"First things first," she said, indicating that Eli should sit next to Levi on the bench. "Before anyone beats anyone else, let's get you strapped in." She explained that these were downhill skis and that cross-country skis would have been more appropriate for the sort of terrain they were on, but she promised this would allow them to get the hang of it.

She started with Eli and showed him how to buckle the boots and snap them into the bindings on the skis.

"Awesome," he said as he stood up. He immediately lost his balance, and Cheryl grabbed him to keep him from falling.

"Whoa there. Slow down. We'll start with something called the snowplow." She handed him the set of ski poles, and he took them and eagerly pushed away from the bench. Well, fine. She'd been planning on starting with basics, like walking in skis, but let him experiment while she helped Levi get set up.

"He seems excited about this," Cheryl said, nodding toward Eli.

"Yes. He is young," Levi said.

Cheryl helped Levi strap his boots into the binding on the skis, explaining that he needed to be sure he heard it click.

"You're not excited?" Cheryl asked.

"I think this will be fun," Levi said. "But mostly, I am glad to be able to spend time with you." He was looking at her so intensely that Cheryl had to look away, remembering that his brother was just feet away and no doubt the whole family was watching through the window.

"Let's try standing up." She held out her hand, and he took it gently and then leaned his weight against her as he got used to the feeling of standing on the skis. She handed him the ski poles and helped him position them outside the skis. She desperately wished she could take a picture of this, but she knew Levi would not appreciate it. The Amish did not document every moment of their lives like everyone else seemed to these days.

"Now. Let's start with walking in skis. Try picking up your feet."

He lifted one foot awkwardly but kept his balance by leaning on the pole. Then he lifted the other.

"Good," Cheryl said, nodding. "That's great. Keep practicing that." She turned and looked for Eli and saw that he had already figured out how to push himself forward using the poles and was gliding around on the packed snow of the yard. It looked awkward, but he was doing it.

"Now, if you need to go up a hill, it's probably easiest to put your skis on a diagonal, like a V," she said as Eli came to a rise in the yard.

"Got it." He was halfway up already.

"He seems like a natural," Cheryl said and turned back to Levi, who grimaced and nodded. He was still getting used to walking and had been doing well. But, seeing his brother zipping around the yard, Levi planted his poles in the ground and tried pushing himself forward. He moved a little ways and tried it again. The third time, though, his pole nicked the edge of his ski, and the surprise threw him off balance. Before Cheryl could react, Levi went down.

"Are you okay?" She ran to his side.

Levi nodded, but he kept his eyes down. He hadn't been moving very fast, but Cheryl knew it could still hurt to fall on snow.

"Did you hurt anything?"

"No, I do not think so," he said. He started to push himself up, his poles splayed out to the sides, and Cheryl held out her hand to help him. His skis were crossed, so first she helped him straighten them out, and then she helped him stand.

"Let's try it again," she said. Levi nodded, and she recognized the dogged determination she'd seen in his eyes before. When Levi was set on a goal, he would work at it until he accomplished it. Cheryl knew that would help him here. He planted his poles in the ground and started pushing himself forward again.

She turned to look for Eli and saw that he was clear over by the barn already. She couldn't see much in the moonlight, but he seemed to be doing just fine on the packed snow. It would be a different story out on the fields, covered with fresh powder, she knew. She didn't know of any groomed trails nearby, so the land around here would have to do for now.

"Come back this way," she called, and he expertly picked up his feet, careful not to cross the skis, and turned himself around. She held her breath as he hit the downhill slope that he'd walked up earlier, but somehow he instinctively knew to make his skis form an inverted V in front of him. It looked like Eli had figured out the snowplow on his own.

A thud from behind her made Cheryl turn. Levi had fallen again. One of his skis had fallen off, and she retrieved it, and then she went over and helped him up, but he wouldn't meet her eye.

She helped him click his boot back into the ski, and she thought she saw a blush creep up his cheeks, but it was hard to tell in the dim light.

"Keep working at it. It's tricky," Cheryl said. Levi nodded but didn't say anything, just pushed off again. She explained the snowplow to him, and he nodded, but it didn't seem to change much.

Both men continued to practice for a while. Levi seemed to be getting the hang of it, she thought. His shoulders were hunched, and he seemed to be bracing at every moment for a fall, but he was getting steadier on his feet. And Eli… Cheryl watched him glide around the yard. Eli seemed made for this. She wondered what might have been if he hadn't been born Amish. Would he have been a ski champion? She could see him hitting the slopes in racing gear, doing moguls or jumps. Maybe he could snowboard, tackle the half-pipe. Could he try to get into those things now? Might Eli be the first Amish ski jumper?

She was pulled from her musing by the sound of Levi falling again.

"I am fine," he said, but there was an edge in his voice she hadn't heard before. He muttered something in Pennsylvania Dutch that she didn't understand and then, refusing her offer of help, hauled himself back to his feet.

"I think I am done for tonight," he said.

"That's a good idea. You had a great first lesson," she said and realized her voice sounded a bit too enthusiastic, a bit forced. "Eli, let's bring it in."

He whistled in response and then started heading back. Levi made his way over to the bench and sat down, and he unclipped the skis.

"It's tough, but you did great," she said, and he nodded.

"This is awesome," Eli said, zipping up next to them. He held his poles out in front of him and used them to hit the house to stop himself. They'd need to work on stopping, apparently. Still, he was doing very well for his first time on skis. She glanced from Eli to his older brother. Was it just the falls that were making Levi grumpy? she wondered. Or was part of his dark mood the fact that his brother seemed to be picking it up so easily? "When can we do this again?"

"I'll come back over again soon," she said. Eli plopped down on the picnic bench and unclipped his boots. "And I can leave them here in case you want to practice without me."

"Yes. Good," Eli said. He banged the ski poles together to get the snow off. Levi seemed to be having a tough time getting one of his boots off the ski, but she wanted to let him work it out if that's what he wanted to do. Cheryl tried to think of a way to take the focus off how differently it had gone for the brothers.

"Eli," Cheryl said, realizing there was something she needed to ask him anyway. "I have been trying to get ahold of Andy Glick. Your mother tells me he's a friend of yours. Do you know if he has a cell phone?"

"Andy?" Eli leaned the poles up against the house. "Why?"

"Your mom said he was here on the day she made the last batch of jam," Cheryl said.

"You think Andy put the poison in the jam?" Eli asked, his eyes wide.

"We're just trying to talk to everyone who was around that day," Cheryl said, trying to keep her voice even. "And I have stopped by his house twice, but he hasn't been around."

"I can give you his phone number. I have it written down inside. But I do not think he poisoned the jam," Eli said, shaking his head.

"He probably didn't," Cheryl said. "But I'd like to talk to him anyway."

"I could see how he might have," Levi said. "Do you remember the time he shaved a stripe in our dog's fur?"

"That was years ago," Eli said. He knocked his boots together to get the snow off. "He's grown up since then."

"It was only a few months ago that he switched out the cinnamon for chili powder in his sister's snickerdoodles," Levi said.

Eli laughed. "Yeah, that is true. But you have to admit that was funny. Half the people at the potluck were walking around chugging ice water."

Cheryl couldn't help chuckling. In her experience, Amish food was not very spicy. Unexpected chili powder would cause quite a stir.

"I did not think it was funny," Levi said. "And neither did his sister. And how many tickets has he gotten for speeding in his sports car the past year?"

"Yeah, but speeding is one thing. Nobody is going to die because you are speeding. But rat poison? He is not that *ab im kopp*."

He's not off in the head, Cheryl silently translated.

"Nobody is going to die?" Levi said. He raised his voice a little, surprising Cheryl. "There are accidents caused by speeding all the time. How many buggies were hit by speeding cars in the past year?"

Cheryl tried to figure out whether Levi was worked up because of the topic or because he was already upset. It was very difficult to know.

"But he has not caused one," Eli said. "Look, I am not saying he always makes good decisions. I know that he does not. But I do believe that not even Andy is silly enough to misunderstand what could happen when you add rat poison to jam."

"Well, someone was silly enough, and now the police are coming to talk to our mother about it," Levi said. "So if it was not Andy, who was it?"

Cheryl felt the tension between them growing, but she didn't know how to stop it. And she knew in a way she could never articulate that this tension wasn't simply about Andy.

"How would I know?" Eli said. "Maybe it was that Englisch girl who makes jam. Maybe she poisoned it to give herself a chance to get jam on the shelves. She knows her jam isn't as good as Maam's."

"That is ridiculous," Levi said.

"What? It is as likely as Andy messing with the jam. More likely, I think."

"She wasn't there the day Maam made the jam. Andy was."

"She could have found a way to poison it."

"You think that Englisch girl would poison the jam and then come over here and chat with Maam like nothing was wrong?" Levi said, shaking his head.

"I did not say it was her, just that it was as likely as Andy..."

Cheryl needed to stop this. "Who is the English girl?" she asked.

Both of them looked up at her like they'd forgotten she was there.

"She's married to this man who has been helping us set up a wireless network," Levi said.

Cheryl almost laughed but managed to stop herself. "A wireless network?" For what?

"It is for the petting zoo," Eli said, as if reading her mind. "So people can pay with credit cards. We will have it running by the time we open again in the spring. This Englisch guy is a computer expert."

"He has been great," Levi said, glaring at Eli. "And his wife is nice."

Eli shrugged. "Does not mean she could not have done it."

"Why don't we head inside?" Cheryl said brightly. She would ask Naomi about this English jam maker, though she had to agree with Levi that it didn't sound like she'd had the opportunity. For now, Cheryl thought it was best to stop this bickering.

Levi stood up. "That is a good idea." He set the skis so they rested against the wall of the house, and then he turned to Cheryl. "Thank you for teaching us, Cheryl." He held her eyes just long enough to make her insides melt, and then he knocked his boots against the step and walked inside.

Cheryl went inside behind Levi and Eli, unsettled. She'd never seen Levi like this. And when she got her boots off and stepped inside, neither Naomi nor Levi were anywhere to be seen.

"He went upstairs," Eli said, downing a large glass of milk. Then, a bit more kindly, "Thank you for teaching us tonight. We both really liked it, and we are thankful."

"Thank you, Eli."

Eli nodded and set his glass down on the counter. He reached into a kitchen drawer and pulled out a small black notebook. "Do you have a pen? Here is Andy's number."

Cheryl took her phone from her jacket pocket and entered the number he read off. Then she tucked it back in and thanked him. There was silence for a moment, and then Eli added, "He will be fine. He is used to being the best at everything. I think it was a shock to see that he was not naturally amazing at skiing too. But when he calms down, he will be fine."

Cheryl thanked him, and then she decided she would give the family space. She would ask Naomi about the English jam maker tomorrow. She said good-bye to Esther and Elizabeth and went outside. The whole way home, she prayed for Levi, for Eli, and for the whole Miller family. But she prayed especially hard for Levi.

CHAPTER ELEVEN

The next morning Cheryl nearly choked on her bagel when she saw the headline in the newspaper: Amish Woman Denies She Poisoned Jam; Four Still in Hospital. Cheryl had slept late this morning after a restless night, and she'd decided to grab breakfast at the Honey Bee and eat it as she opened up the shop. Heather was dong a fine job running the place while Kathy recovered. Heather told her she was coming home from the hospital today, and Cheryl was glad to hear it. Cheryl had also grabbed a copy of the newspaper, which Kathy sold there, but she hadn't really looked at it until she sat down on a stool at the counter inside the shop.

She read the article quickly once and then again more slowly. It said that four people were still recovering, including a state senator's wife. It also made it clear that the senator was demanding justice. The piece named Naomi and also the Swiss Miss, the Honey Bee, and Yoder's Corner. Oh dear. This would not be good for the businesses along Main Street. Cheryl's favorite line was at the end of the article: "When reached by this paper, jam maker Naomi Miller declined to comment."

Which meant that the reporter did not speak Pennsylvania Dutch, she decided. Cheryl finished her bagel and brushed her hands together to get the sesame seeds off her fingers.

Well, she just needed to get this thing solved, now more than ever. Her first order of business, after she turned the sign on the front door to Open, was calling Andy. She pulled out her phone and dialed the number Eli had given her the night before. She held her breath while it rang.

"Hello?" a voice asked. Cheryl felt a jolt of excitement. She'd finally reached him.

"Hi. Is this Andy?"

"Yeah...," he said warily. She heard the sound of a low radio in the background.

"Hi, Andy. This is Cheryl Cooper. I'm a friend of Eli Miller's."

"Yeah?"

"I was hoping I could talk to you for a few minutes. Do you have any time today?"

"About what?"

She should have prepared for this question. She thought quickly. Then she simply decided to go for vagueness.

"I'm helping Eli's mother Naomi on something. She thought you might be able to help."

He sighed. "I'm on my way to work. I work at the big supermarket out on Route 39. I'll have a break about eleven thirty. If you meet me there, I can talk to you then."

"That sounds perfect." Cheryl checked that she had the right store and then quickly thanked him before he hung up. Well, that was a start.

Next she turned on the computer and waited while it booted up. Then she opened a browser window and tried a search she hadn't done the day before. Instead of searching for Stan McCullough's name, she searched directly for the phone number his father had given her. Sure enough, that search turned up a page where you could find out who a phone number was registered to. The number yielded the name Stan McCullough and an address a little ways outside of New Philadelphia.

A handful of customers trickled in before Lydia showed up for her shift, but then Cheryl grabbed her purse, waved good-bye, and headed out. She programmed the address into her phone and found it easily—a well-kept, white double-wide trailer on a small rise, surrounded by several acres of yard.

Cheryl pulled up in front of the house and parked in the small plowed driveway. There was a car in the driveway. She took a deep breath, climbed out of her car, and walked up the wooden steps to the front door. She knocked. She heard movement inside, footsteps coming toward the door. She held her breath. Then the door opened, and a man stood in the doorway. He was tall, with graying brown hair cropped close to his head. He wore a baggy T-shirt that stretched over his belly and jeans. Cheryl noticed he had tattoos all up and down his arms. Maybe it was a bad idea to come here by herself.

"Hi," Cheryl said brightly, pasting a smile on her face. "I'm looking for Stan McCullough."

"That's me." The man's voice was deep but not unkind.

"Hi," Cheryl said again. "My name is Cheryl Cooper, and your father gave me your information."

He tilted his head, waiting for her to go on.

"I'm a good friend of Naomi Miller, and I understand you repaired a propane-powered freezer for her about a month ago."

He thought for a minute, and then he nodded. "That's the farm with a petting zoo?"

"That's right." Cheryl tried to gauge his reaction, watching for any signs of guilt or wariness, but there weren't any. "I was wondering if I could ask you a few questions about that."

"Was there a problem with the freezer?" he asked. If she wasn't mistaken, it seemed like there was genuine concern on his face.

"No, nothing like that," Cheryl said. "I'm just trying to make sense of a few things that happened at her house that day, and I wondered if you might remember anything odd."

Again, there was no sign of guilt or even recognition that he knew what she was talking about. But that didn't mean anything, Cheryl reminded herself. This man was a hardened criminal. He'd been sent to jail for poisoning. He no doubt had plenty of experience hiding what he was really thinking.

"Why don't you come in?" he said and opened the door a bit wider. Cheryl's first reaction was triumph, but it was quickly overshadowed by a wave of fear. Why hadn't she told anyone where she was going? Could she send a quick text to someone to let them know where to look for her if she didn't come back?

"Thank you," she said, trying to sound braver than she felt. She went up the steps, and he held the door open for her as she stepped inside. She looked around. She didn't know what she'd expected, but it wasn't this. The walls were painted a bright clean white, and they were hung with old black-and-white movie posters.

The furniture was cheap, but it all matched, and the beige carpet was clean and looked almost like new. Beyond the living room, she could see a spotless kitchen with white appliances and a small wooden table.

"Have a seat," he said, gesturing toward the couches.

She looked at the clean beige carpet and then the row of shoes lined up by the door. She slipped her shoes off and then padded to the couch under the front window.

"I was just about to have some coffee," he said. "Would you like some too?"

"No," she said a little too forcefully. She didn't have a death wish, thank you very much. He paused for a moment, gave her a strange look, and then nodded and went into the kitchen. She watched as he poured coffee from the carafe of a small coffeemaker into a mug with an eagle on it, and then he stirred in milk and sugar and returned to where she was sitting. He sat on a blue armchair and set his coffee down on a low coffee table.

"So what is it you wanted to know?"

Cheryl tried to think of how she could address this gracefully.

"Can you tell me what you remember about the day you fixed my friend Naomi's freezer?" Cheryl asked.

"Sure." He picked up his coffee and took a sip. "I don't remember much, to be honest. One of her kids, a teenage girl, answered the door, and then your friend showed me downstairs. She was busy cooking something in the kitchen, if I remember right. Anyway, I took a look at the freezer, and it was pretty easy to see that the flame spreader was busted, so I went back out to my truck and replaced it with a spare I had, and that was that. It was a pretty quick fix."

"How long would you say you were there?"

He shrugged. "Two hours, tops?"

"During how much of that time were you alone in the basement?"

"Most of it probably. Why?"

Cheryl didn't answer that question, but asked another.

"Did you explore the basement much while you were there?"

"Nothing really sticks out in my mind." He took another sip of his coffee and set it down. "Now can I ask you something?"

Cheryl didn't know what else to do, so she nodded.

"Do these questions have anything to do with the article I read in the paper this morning about rat poison in the jam your friend made?"

Cheryl nodded again.

He let out a breath. "And can I assume that you're asking me these questions because you did some background research on me?"

Cheryl didn't know what else to do but nod. "And because you were one of very few people who were there the day the jam was made," Cheryl said, lifting up her chin.

He seemed honestly incredulous. He shook his head. "The jam was poisoned the day I was there?"

"Someone added rat poison before she sealed the jars," Cheryl said. "Which means it had to have been that day you were there."

"Wow." He sighed. "If that's the case, I can see why you would think of me. But please believe me when I say this: I don't know anything about that. I didn't even realize it was jam she was making that day. I wouldn't have the slightest idea where to find rat poison. I had no reason to do anything like that. I wouldn't do that. I *didn't* do it."

Cheryl wanted to believe the earnestness in his voice. But just because he acted like he'd had nothing to do with it didn't mean he hadn't.

"You have been arrested for poisoning before, isn't that right?" Cheryl asked.

He cringed, shook his head, and then said, "Yes. It was a long time ago. I am a different person now."

"You put antifreeze in someone's coffee."

He sighed. "Look. I'm not denying I did it. I was young and stupid, and I did something ridiculous. Something horrible. I was jealous, angry, and hateful, and I did a very bad thing." He picked up his coffee cup and turned it around in his hands. "And I served my time for it. In some ways, going to prison was the best thing that ever happened to me."

"How so?"

His voice had lost its edge. "For one thing, it got me away from some people I should not have been around in the first place." He took a sip, and she could see that his hands were shaking. "For another, I found the Lord in prison."

"So you're a Christian?"

"Yes, ma'am. Washed in the blood." He held out his arm, and she saw that one of the tattoos on his forearm was of a large cross. "There was this chaplain who came to visit. He and I got to talking, and over a period of many months, I became convinced that God was real, that Jesus was real, and that grace was real. I asked the Lord to come into my heart and make me a new person. And I know that I can never make it right, what I did, but I also know that I am forgiven."

Cheryl loved stories like this. Stories where God's grace shone through and a sinner became redeemed. And as Cheryl looked around, she noticed that the books on the side table next to the couch were Christian titles, including a well-worn leather-bound Bible. She thought there was a good chance that he was telling the truth about his newfound faith.

But Cheryl also knew that Christians did bad things all the time. Becoming a believer didn't free him of temptation or break bad patterns.

"I go to Grace Church, over off Route 416. You know it?"

Cheryl shook her head.

"It's a good church. The pastor knows a lot about the Bible. He is big on living as lights in the world. How about you? Are you a Christian?"

Cheryl nodded. "I used to go to Silo Church, and now I go to Friendship Mennonite."

"I've heard those are both good places. Well, see, then you know."

Cheryl nodded, not committing one way or the other. Sure, she wanted to believe him. She wanted to have faith in another believer. And he seemed honest and forthright to her. But given the circumstances, it was hard to discount the fact that he was the only non-Amish person who'd had the opportunity to poison the jam. And given what Cheryl knew about the tight bonds in the Amish community, it was much easier to believe that someone not Amish had committed a crime like this.

"I know it looks bad. But I promise you that I don't know anything about this. I have no motive, no reason to do something like this, right?"

Cheryl nodded, though she couldn't be sure. She couldn't think of any reason he would have done it, but that didn't mean he didn't have one.

"I can see I can't convince you. But here. Let me give you the number of my pastor, Matt Brown. He'll vouch for me." He set down the coffee and pushed himself up. "I might have done something stupid like that when I was younger, but not now. He'll tell you."

Cheryl took the paper he held out to her. She would talk to his pastor. But she would still look for evidence to prove it one way or another.

She stood up to go. "Thank you for talking with me."

"Of course." He led her to the door. "I'll be praying that the real culprit comes to light."

She nodded and hurried out to her car, more confused than ever. Instead of calling Matt Brown, Cheryl decided to stop by the church and see if he was around. She found the church easily enough, a white stucco building right on Route 416, just outside the main town area of New Philadelphia. She parked in the large empty lot. Judging by the size of the parking lot, this place was hopping on Sunday mornings, but on a Thursday morning, it was all but empty. The few cars were clustered at the far end of the lot, so Cheryl parked down that way and guessed that was where the office was. Jackpot. There were glass doors on the side of the building, with a small sign that said Office over it. Cheryl pushed open the door and stepped into a hallway, with the office just off that to the right. The whole place was covered in a turquoise-green carpet, and the walls were painted a tan color. She was greeted by an enthusiastic woman with frosted blonde hair.

"Welcome to Grace Church. How can I help you?"

"I was wondering if I could talk to Pastor Matt Brown," Cheryl said.

"Do you have an appointment?"

Behind the small front office, there were offices that branched off behind heavy oak doors.

"No, I'm afraid not. I wanted to ask him about one of his congregants, Stan McCullough."

"Oh, Stan." The woman's smile got wider. "He's wonderful, isn't he?" She turned and looked at something on her screen. Cheryl leaned in a bit and saw that it was a calendar. "Well, Pastor Matt doesn't have anything on his calendar right now. Let me see if he's free."

Cheryl nodded and stepped back while the woman used her phone to place a call. Then she looked up and smiled. "He has a lunch meeting in a few minutes, but he's free for a little bit if you want to go back." She gestured to the doors behind her. "It's the second door on the right."

"Thank you." Cheryl walked down the hallway toward the door the secretary had indicated, and she knocked gently on the mostly closed door.

"Come in."

She pushed open the heavy door and saw a man in a button-down shirt and dress pants look up from a computer and smile at her.

"Hello. Come in, come in." He gestured for her to step in and sit down. She lowered herself into a padded chair. The room held a desk and a large bookshelf stuffed with books. The wood matched the door and the desks in the front office, and the carpet continued throughout. "I'm Matt Brown."

"Hello, Pastor. I'm Cheryl Cooper. I run the Swiss Miss over in Sugarcreek."

"It's nice to meet you, Cheryl. And please call me Matt."

"Thank you. And thanks for taking the time to meet with me today."

He nodded. "Sheila said you want to talk about Stan McCullough?"

The pastor was probably in his late forties, and he had thinning brown hair and glasses and a genuine smile.

"That's right. I was wondering if you could tell me a bit about him."

"Stan is a wonderful man. A huge asset to our congregation." He paused and looked at Cheryl. "Can I ask why you want to know about Stan?"

Cheryl quickly explained the basics: the jam, the fact that he'd been there that day, that she was trying to figure out what happened.

"Ah," Matt said. "I see."

Cheryl waited for him to go on. "You see?"

"I see why you are looking into him. But I can tell you this: I have never seen a man more changed than Stanley McCullough. His mother has come to this church for years, and I had met him a number of times when he was growing up. When he went to prison, it nearly killed her. But something happened to him in prison. He changed, deep down in his heart. When he got out, Stan started coming here too, and he was like a different person. The old has gone, the new has come."

Cheryl understood the reference to Second Corinthians 5:17: "Therefore, if anyone is in Christ, the new creation has come: The old has gone, the new is here!"

"So you're saying his faith seems genuine to you?"

"As much as it's possible to tell about another person's faith, yes. And I don't think he would have put poison into your friend's jam."

His phone rang, and the secretary announced that his lunch companion was here.

Cheryl thanked him and stood to go, and as she walked back out to her car, she puzzled over what this meant. It didn't prove anything. Just because Stan McCullough's pastor didn't think he could have done it didn't mean that he was innocent. Didn't pastors have to see the best in people? It was sort of a job requirement.

But as Cheryl climbed into her car, she had to admit that she kind of believed him too. She believed that Jesus changed hearts, and she believed that it wasn't fair to hold someone's past mistakes against them now. Her sense was that Stan had been speaking to her genuinely. But again, it wasn't proof.

Well, she'd keep looking, but Stan had fallen from the top perch on her suspect list. *Speaking of which...* Cheryl glanced at the clock and saw that it was almost time to meet up with Andy Glick. She backed out of the parking space and drove through the empty lot to the exit on the far side, and then she started to drive back toward Sugarcreek. A few miles outside of town, she came to the shopping center that held the big chain grocery store she used for big shopping trips.

She pulled into a spot at the side of the store and walked in the sliding front door. Cheryl walked past the bakery, with its glistening cakes and pastries, through the produce section, past piles of tomatoes and grapefruit that let off the most heavenly scent, looking for Andy. He hadn't said where to meet him. How would she know what he looked like? She gave up and asked the woman at the first check-out lane, and she directed Cheryl toward the aisle. "He's stocking shelves," she said. "I think I saw him headed to aisle three a few minutes ago. Short brown hair, brown eyes. Tall. You'll find him."

Cheryl thanked her and headed to aisle three, and sure enough she found Andy restocking shelves in the cereal aisle. He matched the description the woman had given him, and he wore a name tag pinned to his black apron that said Andy.

"Hey," he said. He set a box of Lucky Charms onto the shelf and turned to her. Cheryl's mouth watered. She knew it was like eating a bowl of candy in the morning, but she loved that stuff. "You must be Cheryl."

"Yes. And you're Andy," she said, gesturing toward his name tag.

"I'm just about done here. Hang on one second." He reached into the cardboard box at his feet and pulled out two more boxes of the cereal and put them on the shelf. Then he picked up the empty cardboard box, broke it down expertly, and indicated she should follow him. She walked behind him down to the end of the aisle, past the case of prepackaged meat, and through a swinging door marked Employees Only.

"Is it okay that I'm back here?" Cheryl asked. The ceilings were high, and beyond a few rooms right by the door, the space was dark and piled high with boxes and pallets of food.

"It's fine," he said. He tossed the flattened box onto a pile and ushered her inside one of the small rooms. She quickly saw that it was an employee break room, with a refrigerator and white cabinets and a microwave and a small table. Fluorescent overhead lights popped and buzzed and cast everything in a sickly light. Andy waved at a woman eating macaroni and cheese from a microwave dish and then gestured for Cheryl to sit. "You want coffee?" he asked.

Cheryl shook her head, but he went to a machine that made single cups and slipped in a plastic pod of dark roast. A minute later, he had a steaming cup of coffee, and he sat down in one of the plastic chairs across from her.

"So. Eli gave you my number?" he asked. Cheryl nodded, and she opened her mouth, but before she could speak, he said, "If you're here about that horse for sale, the price is firm. I am not going down. She's a good horse."

"Oh. No, I'm not here about a horse," Cheryl said. "I've been trying to get in touch with you for a few days. I went to your house."

"You did?" He shrugged. "No one told me. What did you want to talk to me about if not the horse?"

"I've actually heard that you like to play practical jokes," Cheryl said. He looked at her warily, his hands wrapped around the paper cup.

"Yes?"

"I was wondering if there was any chance you might have played a joke at Eli's house recently?"

He stared at her, probably trying to decide what to make of her. "Not that I can remember."

"You didn't play a practical joke? One involving jam?"

"Jam?" He screwed up his face. "What kind of joke involves jam?"

"It's okay to be honest. I'm not looking to get anyone in trouble. I'm just trying to figure out the truth."

"Okay." He shook his head. "But the truth is, I really don't know anything about jam. I have no idea what you're talking about."

Cheryl studied him. He seemed genuine. But then, so had everyone she'd talked to so far. And one of them had to have put the rat poison into that jam. There were a limited number of people who could have had access to it the day Naomi was making it.

"Do you know what rat poison does?" Cheryl asked.

He looked at her like she was nuts. "Um, it kills rats?" He shook his head. "I grew up on a farm, you know. I know what rat poison is for."

"Is there any chance you might have found some at Eli's house a few weeks ago?"

"What?" He shook his head. "No. I don't know what you're implying, but no. I have not touched rat poison at Eli's house, ever. I really don't know what you're talking about." He took a sip of the coffee. "Now, if that's all, I have to get back to work."

With that, he scooted his chair back, and Cheryl stood.

"Thank you for taking the time to talk to me," she said.

He nodded, and Cheryl hooked her purse over her arm and found her own way out while he remained sitting at the table.

As she drove back to the Swiss Miss, Cheryl puzzled over the encounter. He'd seemed honestly confused by her questions. But maybe he was a good actor? She didn't know what to believe anymore.

Chapter Twelve

Cheryl arrived back at the Swiss Miss a few minutes later, and she greeted Lydia and Esther.

"How did it go while I was gone?" Cheryl asked. She set her purse down under the counter and rested a paper bag that held a sandwich she'd picked up at the Honey Bee on the counter. She found out from Heather that Kathy was home now. Cheryl would try to stop by and bring her a meal in the next few days.

"Terrible. Everything fell apart without you," Lydia said.

Cheryl had been taking the sandwich out of the bag, but now she looked up and glanced at Lydia. The shop looked okay, the shelves stocked and neat and orderly.

"What do you mean?"

Lydia waited a beat before she laughed. "I am just kidding, Cheryl. Everything was fine. There have only been a few customers all day. We have it under control."

"Oh, good." Cheryl reached back into the bag and pulled out her sandwich. "Don't scare me like that."

The Amish girls both laughed, and then they went back to dusting. Cheryl was glad things were quiet here because that meant she didn't feel guilty taking off to learn what she could about the jam, but she did worry about the fact that the shop had been so quiet the past few days. Surely it was just because it was the middle of the week in a quiet time of year, she thought. She tried to reassure herself that it was nothing more than that. The article linking the tainted jam to the store couldn't be the reason foot traffic was down, could it?

Cheryl shook her head. It was too early to say. For now, she sat down on the stool and bit into her sandwich gratefully. She hadn't realized how hungry she was. As she chewed, she gazed out the window at the drifts of snow blowing about in the breeze. She thought about what she'd realized last night, about how ski resorts make their own snow. How did they do that? Was there any way she could do the same on a smaller scale? Or, more accurately, send Aunt Mitzi the tools she would need to make it?

Cheryl turned to her computer and shook the mouse to wake it up. Then she did a search for the phrase "make your own snow."

Huh. There were instructions for making fake snow using baking powder and shaving cream on a page for homeschooling ideas. The result was meant to look like snow, but it wouldn't melt or have the same feel as the real thing. Plus, it would be difficult to make enough of it to give Mitzi the feel of experiencing a snowfall. Cheryl clicked back and saw that you could buy home snow-making equipment. They were basically smaller versions of what the ski resorts used, and you could use them to coat your own yard. Then she saw the price. Were there really people who had so much money they would pay that price to make their backyard wintry? Cheryl shook her head. It was a nice idea, but it was not going to work to ship one of those things to Aunt Mitzi.

Then she found a page that told you how to make your own snow with a power washer and a garden hose. Which was all fine, except who had a power washer? And even if she did have one, it would be prohibitively expensive to ship something like that halfway around the world. And while she believed that some of these ideas might work here in Ohio when it was chilly out, she had a hard time believing even a commercial-grade gadget could make real snow in a place like Papua New Guinea, where they had beach weather every day. She clicked back to the main search page and kept looking.

"Cheryl?"

Cheryl looked up to see Ben Vogel standing in front of her. From the look on his face, she guessed he'd called her name more than once.

"Oh. Hi, Ben."

"Hello." He smiled. "Absorbed in something interesting?"

"Just trying to figure out how to make snow."

"That's funny." He pulled his hat off and brushed some white flakes off of it. "The rest of us are trying to figure out how to make it stop."

"Fair enough." She laughed. "So what's going on?"

"I was just talking with a friend of mine who works at the hospital over in Dover," Ben said. "You'd heard that there were two more patients admitted for poisoning, right?"

Cheryl nodded. "Did he have any news on them? Are they okay?"

"Actually, yes, he did tell me some news," Ben said. "One of them, the Amish girl, is recovering well. They hope she will be home with her family shortly."

"Thank goodness." Cheryl knew the family would have large bills to deal with, but at least their daughter was safe. "And the other man?"

"Well, that's where it gets interesting," Ben said. "See, when he was admitted, he showed the same signs as the others who had eaten the jam. And since the Amish girl had been admitted just shortly before, after having jam at Yoder's Corner, they asked if he had eaten there as well. When he said he had, the doctors assumed it must be the same thing that was making him sick."

"But it wasn't?" Cheryl didn't even want to allow herself to hope that one of the cases wasn't from poisoned jam after all.

"They treated him like it was, and at first he responded the same way. But then he took a turn for the worse, and they weren't sure why. Well, after they'd talked to him some, they found out that he'd gotten worse after he'd taken a dose of his anticoagulant."

"His what?" Cheryl had heard that term in the past few days, she was sure of it.

"His blood-thinning medication. He was taking several medications after a heart attack last year, and one was a blood thinner, warfarin. It is often called by the brand name Coumadin. People take it to prevent blood clots and that sort of thing. But it turns out he'd missed a few doses, so he tried to make up for it by taking three doses of this medication at once."

"Oh dear." Cheryl saw where this was going. She'd heard the name warfarin before. "That's an ingredient in rat poison, isn't it?"

"It is indeed. In small doses, it's perfectly safe and often saves lives. But like any medication, if you take too large of a dose, there can be complications."

"And in this case, the complications looked a whole lot like the poison for the jam."

He nodded. "My guess is that if there hadn't already been three patients who'd eaten poisoned jam in the past few days, they would have picked up on what it really was right away. But since the symptoms were so like the others, and since he had eaten at Yoder's Corner, it was an easy mistake to make."

Cheryl thought about the implications of this turn of events. So at least one of the four who'd been poisoned hadn't actually been poisoned after all. Was there any chance... No, Kathy didn't take a blood thinner. And certainly the healthy young Amish girl didn't. Besides which, Ben had had the jam tested chemically, and he had found traces of the rat poison in it. So she couldn't assume the others might have taken overdoses of their medications also.

But still, it was one fewer person hurt by the jam. One less person who could bring a lawsuit, she thought ruefully. And the man whose wife had bought the jam at the Swiss Miss was still talking about suing.

"I just thought you might want to know," Ben said, ducking his head.

"Yes, I do. Thank you for telling me."

"Of course." He was twisting his knit hat in his hands. "Okay, well, I'm meeting Rueben here in a bit, so I'll just go over there and wait."

"Thank you, Ben. I really appreciate it."

"Anytime."

Cheryl finished her sandwich and was just cleaning up the crumbs she'd spilled on the counter when the door opened again. Cheryl expected to see Rueben Vogel shuffle inside, but she was surprised when it was Chief Twitchell who came in once again. This time the police chief was trailed by Officer Ortega, whom Cheryl recognized from previous cases she'd been involved with.

"Afternoon, Cheryl," the police chief said in his Southern drawl. Officer Ortega touched her cap in greeting.

"Hello, Chief Twitchell. Officer Ortega." Cheryl tried to smile, but she was afraid her wariness was evident. What were they doing here again?

"We were hopin' you could tell us a bit more about the jam that was sold at your shop the other day," Chief Twitchell said.

"The jam?" She narrowed her eyes. "I already told you about the jam. You took the jar."

"Yes, but we're trying to figure out if anything unusual might have happened to the jam after it left Naomi's kitchen," Officer Ortega said. "So I wondered what you could tell us about when you put the jam on the shelf and where it was stored before then."

Cheryl tried to figure out what was going on. Was this a trick? What did they mean, asking questions about this?

"Naomi brought in the shipment of jam on Friday. We put the jam on the shelves that day. The stuff is very popular, and we were running low. It only sat on the shelf for a day before it was sold on Saturday."

Officer Ortega made some notes in her notebook. "Do you remember anyone strange coming into the store at any point before the jam was purchased?"

"No." Cheryl was confused by the line of questioning. Did she remember anyone strange in her shop? Why were they asking questions like this? Wasn't it obvious that the jam had been doctored long before it got to her shop?

"You didn't open the jars of jam by chance, did you?" Chief Twitchell asked.

What in the... Cheryl tried to fight the wave of anger that rose up in her. What, did he think she had opened the jar, sprinkled rat poison in, and then put it on her shelf to sell? What could she possibly have to gain from that? Ruining her business and her best friend's reputation?

"Why in the world would I do something like that?" Cheryl asked. Both police officers reared their heads back. And, okay, it might have come out a bit more forcefully than she'd intended it to. But really, what were they thinking? "I'm the one who reported this whole thing to you in the first place, remember?" Cheryl said. "I tried to get you to investigate, but you weren't interested. And now, after someone else reported it as well, someone who apparently has the power to make things happen in this state, now you're accusing *me* of tampering with the jam?"

"I wasn't accusin' you of anything..."

Cheryl cut him off. "You asked if I had opened the jam. No, Chief Twitchell, I did not open the jam. I did not put rat poison in the jam my best friend made and then sell it at the business my aunt built from the ground up and trusted me to run. You're wasting my time and yours when you could be out there trying to find out who the real culprit is."

Neither officer said anything for a moment, and Cheryl used the pause to try to catch her breath. She was vaguely aware that Esther, Lydia, and Ben were all looking at her. Well, it wasn't the first time she'd been accused of having a temper. And it wasn't the first time that she'd said what needed to be said either.

"We weren't trying to make any sort of accusation," Officer Ortega said gently, raising her hands, apparently to show her innocence. "Somehow we got off on the wrong foot. We actually came in to ask..."

"We 'got off on the wrong foot' because you asked if I..."

"Actually, we came in here to ask for your help," Chief Twitchell said quickly.

"My help?" she said, her eyes narrowed. If they were asking for her help, they sure had a strange way of going about it.

He nodded. "When you first came in to talk to me, you mentioned you had a list of people who had had access to the jam the day Naomi was makin' it. I went to speak with Naomi yesterday, and she wouldn't tell me who they were."

"She didn't tell you any of their names?" Why would Naomi try to keep Andy's and Martha's names from the police?

"Well, she gave us one. A freezer repairman. We tracked him down, and it turned out you'd already spoken to him when we got there a few hours ago."

"I hadn't even known the Amish used freezers," Officer Ortega said, shrugging. She was trying too hard to lull her into relaxing, Cheryl thought.

"And what did he tell you?" Cheryl asked.

"No doubt the same thing he told you. That he had nothin' to do with it."

"And do you believe him?"

"What I need to know are the names of the other people on your list," Chief Twitchell said.

He hadn't answered her question, Cheryl noticed. But there was something more interesting she needed to figure out.

"Did Naomi say why she wouldn't give you the other names?"

"No." He shook his head. "But I assumed it was because they were Amish. You know how they are about the police in their culture."

It was true, Cheryl did know. They tried to avoid bringing in the police whenever they could. And if Naomi had wanted to protect the identity of the two Amish people she'd talked to, Cheryl thought she probably should too. Still, Cheryl took a moment of sweet enjoyment at the idea of the police asking her for help.

"But the thing is, if we don't find out who really did tamper with the jam, Naomi is going to be the one liable," Officer Ortega said. "So if you do know of anyone who might be able to shed some light on things, it would be wise to tell us who they are."

Cheryl thought about this for a moment. She didn't want Naomi to get in trouble.

"We're gettin' a lot of pressure from the outside to wrap up this case quickly," Chief Twitchell said. Cheryl understood what he was saying. The state senator was pushing him to make an arrest. She recognized the veiled threat in there—if he was forced to make an arrest, it would be Naomi. But they both knew that Naomi wasn't behind the poison, so he wanted her help to come up with the other suspects.

Again, there was a certain amount of thrill about the fact that he needed her help after all. But when she put that aside, Cheryl wasn't sure what to do. She didn't want Naomi arrested. Nor did she want to betray her trust. Finally, Cheryl made a decision. If it came down to it and Naomi was in imminent danger, Cheryl would give the police Andy's and Martha's names. But she wouldn't do it before then, not if it could be avoided. And in the meantime, she'd keep looking for the real culprit herself.

"I'm sorry, I don't know," Cheryl said as sweetly as she could.

The police didn't believe her, that was clear. But after assuring them a few times that she couldn't tell them the names of the Amish people they sought, there was nothing more they could do.

"This isn't a joke, Cheryl," Chief Twitchell said as he and Officer Ortega left. "Naomi could be in real trouble if this thing escalates any further."

Cheryl let those words settle over her. Yes, Naomi could be in real trouble. But she already was. And Cheryl was going to make sure she got out of it as soon as possible.

CHAPTER THIRTEEN

After the police left, Cheryl sat on a stool at the counter and spent some time thinking over what she knew about her suspects. A day ago, she'd have put her money on Stan McCullough as the culprit. But after talking to him and his pastor, she wasn't convinced about that. He had the opportunity, and his history made him an obvious suspect. Yet his repentance seemed genuine, and his pastor truly believed he was changed. Plus, as far as Cheryl could see, he had no motive.

Andy Glick had also seemed a likely option. But when she'd talked to him today, he seemed genuinely confused by her questions. It was possible he was simply a good actor, but that would make him the first Broadway-ready Amish man she'd ever met. Plus, from what she could tell, he definitely did like to play practical jokes that were often not appreciated by the victims, but she hadn't heard of anything he'd done that would endanger people like this. Andy may be a jokester with poor judgment, but he'd grown up on a farm. He knew the dangers of rat poison.

Which left little Martha. Was it possible the girl really had brought up rat poison instead of pectin? It seemed unlikely she'd mix the two up. Still, it seemed the likeliest scenario at this point.

Cheryl picked up a pen and tapped it against the counter. There had to be more possibilities. Then she remembered something Eli had said last night, about the English girl who made jam. He'd thought she was a possibility, while Levi thought that was crazy. Cheryl had thought of and tossed out the idea of a rival jam maker as a suspect a few days ago, but now she reconsidered it. Cheryl didn't see how it would work for her to have been behind the poisoning, but she figured it was probably worth at least finding out more about her.

"Esther?"

The girl looked up from the set of place mats she was reorganizing at the other side of the store. Cheryl saw that Lydia was sitting in a chair watching Ben and Rueben play checkers. Well, the girl had done plenty of work in the past few days, and since there were no customers here anyway, Cheryl didn't mind if she relaxed for a bit.

"Can I ask you a few questions?"

"Of course." She set down the stack and made her way to the counter.

"Last night Eli mentioned a woman who makes jam. Her husband has been doing some computer work for your family."

"Ah yes. Bridget. She is sweet. Her husband, Carter, is very good with computers, and the wireless network he is setting up will be so helpful this summer."

"Have you talked with her much?"

"Some. Carter has come to work on setting up the network three or four times. It seems that they only have one car, so when her husband comes to our farm to work, she must drop him off and pick him up. Once or twice she has gone to run errands while he worked, but other times we have invited her in for tea. She seems to like that."

"What can you tell me about her?"

Esther thought for a minute before she spoke. "She is young," she finally said. "I believe they have not been married long. And..." She hesitated. "I think they do not know a lot about living in the country."

"What makes you say that?"

"They recently moved here from Cincinnati, and it did not seem like either of them had lived in anything but a city. When we first talked to her, she used a lot of words like *sustainable* and *eco-friendly* and *off the grid.*"

Cheryl laughed. There was nothing wrong with those words—in fact, in her experience, Amish farms were some of the most sustainable and eco-friendly out there, and they were certainly off the grid—but she could see what Esther was trying to illustrate. When she'd lived in Columbus, a lot of people, especially around the university, talked about moving to the country to live lives more in line with nature and old-fashioned farming practices. They were generally into artisanal everything and typically, in her experience, knew very little about actual farming. "So they are young and idealistic and moved to the country to live a simple life, but don't necessarily understand all that entails."

"Yes, that is about right."

Something about this tickled at the back of her mind. Had she heard about this jam maker before this? Cheryl tried to get her mind to form a memory, but she couldn't.

"Do they have a farm?"

"I think they are planning to plant vegetables and get a goat in the spring."

So they would start small. That was probably a good idea, but they wouldn't be living off that, certainly not at this time of year. "Do you know how they make money?"

"He does the computer work. She does not seem to have a job from what I can tell. She mentioned she does a lot of crafts and sells them on the Internet. Maybe she sells enough to pay the bills? I do not know." She shrugged. "I believe she was hoping to make some money selling jam. But I do not know if this has happened."

Again, something tickled in her mind. She couldn't figure out why, but try as hard as she could, she couldn't bring to mind why this sounded familiar to her.

"What is her name?" Cheryl asked.

"Bridget. Bridget Marshall."

Cheryl turned to the computer and typed the name into an open browser window. The first thing that came up was a Facebook page. Cheryl clicked on it, and she studied the profile picture. The girl had long dark hair and freckles and bright blue eyes. Cheryl had seen her before. She sat back on the stool and stared at the picture. Where had she seen her before?

Then it hit her. She'd met this girl! She had come into the shop. Cheryl closed her eyes and thought for a moment, and slowly it came back to her.

She had come in here a few months back. She stood out from the regular customers because she was wearing skinny jeans and ankle boots and an overly large scarf and thick-framed glasses, and Cheryl's first thought had been that she was glad she didn't have to dress like a city person anymore. The girl looked out of place among tourists and Christmas sweatshirts and Amish girls in long dresses.

That was right, it had been right smack-dab in the middle of the Christmas rush, and there had been a dozen people waiting to check out and fifteen other things that needed to be done. So when this girl came in bearing homemade jam to try to get Cheryl to stock it in the store, Cheryl hadn't really spent much time with her before dismissing her. She already stocked Amish jam, she explained, and it sold quite well, so she wasn't looking for a new supplier. Cheryl thought back. The jam had been some odd flavor, she recalled. Something she hadn't thought would sell well here anyway. People who came to this store liked the idea that the jam had been made by Amish women, and they wanted simple, traditional flavors, not juniper berry or whatever strange— "artisanal," the girl had called it—flavor she had been peddling.

Cheryl tried to remember. What had she done with that jam?

She stood up and walked into the back room, and she rummaged around one of the storage shelves. That's right—there it was. She pulled from where she had shoved it and studied the jar now. It was packed in a mason jar with a cute handwritten label. The jam was white peach and hibiscus flavor. It actually didn't sound bad, but Cheryl didn't think it would sell well around here.

She brought it out to show Esther. "This is her jam, right?"

Esther looked at the jar and nodded. "She brought a few to our house. One was fig with candied ginger, which I did not care for because I do not like the taste of ginger. And the other was blood orange with rosemary. That one was not bad if you could get past the name."

"So you tried her jam?"

"Yes. It was interesting. I could see why she wanted to try to sell it. But I prefer my maam's jam."

Cheryl thought through what this could mean. The girl knew about jam. She had been to the Millers' house. Could she have...

"She didn't stop by the day your mother made the jam, did she?"

Esther shook her head. "No, I do not believe she did. You do not think she might have been behind the rat poison, do you?" Esther's eyes were wide.

"I'm just thinking out loud," Cheryl said.

"She is so sweet. It is hard to imagine that she could hurt a fly," Esther said.

Be that as it may, and as unlikely as it seemed that she could have poisoned the jam, Cheryl thought she should talk to her. Now how would she find out...

Wait. Cheryl went to the back room and yanked out the top desk drawer. There, buried under pens and rubber bands, was the business card the girl had given her back in December. Bridget Marshall, Artisanal Jams, it said, and there was an address and phone number listed.

"I think I'm going to go out for a bit," Cheryl said.

Esther nodded. "I think that is a very *goot* idea."

CHAPTER FOURTEEN

Cheryl ended up giving Esther a ride home since her shift was almost over, and though she scanned the yard for any sign of Levi as Esther climbed out, she didn't see him. She did see Eli, wearing the black skis, zipping around the area behind the house. He waved a pole in greeting. She waved too and then backed up and pulled out of the driveway. She tried not to be disappointed. Levi was no doubt working hard at something. Then she turned and headed toward the address on Bridget's business card.

It was off the beaten path, that was for sure, Cheryl thought as she turned off a winding country road on to a dirt road. It hadn't been plowed, and she was glad her little car had snow tires or she never would have made it. Finally, she pulled up in front of a small yellow and brown bungalow-style house. It was a cute house, though the porch was sagging and it desperately needed a coat of paint. A few acres around the house had been cleared, and beyond that was thick forest. She went as far as her car could go, and she climbed out and headed up the steps to the front door.

She rang the doorbell, but it didn't seem to do anything, so she rapped on the frame of the screen door, and a few moments later she saw the curtain on the front window flutter. Cheryl smiled and tried to look unassuming. A few moments later, the door opened.

The girl stood in front of her, wearing baggy jeans and a fleece over a chunky wool sweater and a knit hat over her long, dark hair.

"Hi," Cheryl said, a little too brightly. "I'm Cheryl Cooper, from the Swiss Miss. Bridget, right? We met a few months ago."

"Yeah." The girl seemed to be leaning on the door for support. Cheryl couldn't tell if it was because she was nervous or whether she was just too skinny. "Hi."

"I hope you don't mind me stopping in, but earlier today I found the jar of jam you brought by, and I wondered if I could talk to you about the jams you make."

"Oh." The girl blinked. "Of course. That'd be great. Please come in." She was sweet, Cheryl thought.

She stepped back, and Cheryl entered the house. The floors creaked as Cheryl stepped inside. The front living room was small, but it was well decorated, with light gray walls and framed prints and cute little statues and objects everywhere. The furniture looked secondhand, or simply well-loved perhaps, but Bridget had added stylish throw pillows. But what Cheryl noticed most of all was how cold it was inside the house. She was surprised she couldn't see her own breath in here.

"Come on in," Bridget said. "I'd offer to take your coat, but honestly you'll probably want to keep it." She grimaced.

"Is the heater broken?"

She laughed uncomfortably. "There's a pellet stove in the kitchen, but it doesn't always reach all the rooms."

Cheryl tried to make sense of this. They couldn't live like this all the time, could they? Winter would be unbearable.

"This place is really cute," Cheryl said, indicating the living room.

"Thanks. We're trying. We just moved in the fall, and we're planning to slowly fix it up. See out there?" She indicated the front yard, covered under a thick layer of snow. "I'm planning to plant a big vegetable garden. And around back there's an old pole barn that we'll clean out and raise goats and maybe chickens." Bridget's eyes lit up as she talked about their plans.

"That will be really nice," Cheryl said, nodding. She saw that opposite the living room was a small bathroom done in outdated sea-foam green tiles and a closet.

"And we have big dreams for the house too. I mean, we've got a long way to go, obviously, but in a few years, I'm hoping we'll have it all fixed up." She smiled. She saw Cheryl glancing at the bathroom. "Starting with the bathroom." She laughed. "Would you like some tea?"

"That would be lovely." If only to stay warm.

"Follow me," she said, and Cheryl walked down the hall, the hardwood floorboards, no doubt original to the house, creaking with every step. "That's the first bedroom," she said, indicating a room piled high with boxes. "Or it will be when we get to unpacking it." She laughed. Cheryl noticed that there was a brown stain on the ceiling of the bedroom. The roof was leaking then.

"And back here is our bedroom and my craft room."

"Craft room?"

"Yeah. Come take a look." She led Cheryl to a small bedroom at the end of the hallway. There was a table with a fluorescent lamp in the middle of the room, and the walls were lined with shelves stacked high with clear storage boxes. "I sell a lot of stuff online. You know Etsy?"

Cheryl nodded. She knew the site where people sold handcrafted items.

"I sell a lot of my stuff there."

"Like what?" Cheryl eyed the plastic boxes, and she saw skeins of yarn and jars of paint and papers piled high.

"Oh, all kinds of stuff. I knit scarves, do calligraphy, make letterpressed cards. That kind of thing." She shrugged. "And, of course, I'm trying to make some money selling my jam."

"Of course." Cheryl tried to think of how to broach the subject she'd come here to discuss, but as she fumbled through her mind looking for openers, Bridget indicated that she should follow her, and they stepped out of the craft room and into the kitchen.

The kitchen was small and boxy, with a laminate counter and wooden cabinets that seemed to be left over from the sixties. But Bridget had changed out the hardware, installing modern-looking glass knobs, and it gave the room a more contemporary feel. But the main thing Cheryl noticed was the pellet stove in the corner of the room. It was at least ten degrees warmer in here, and the air was tinged with a sweet smell. Bridget filled a blue-green teakettle and set it on the stove.

"So. You wanted to ask about my jam?" She turned on the gas on the old-fashioned stove, and a flame leaped to life under the teakettle.

"Yes." Cheryl thought quickly. "You mentioned you're looking to make money selling jam. Can you remind me of the sort of jam you make?"

"Of course." She pulled down two mugs from a cabinet and set them on the counter. "I used my grandmother's recipes but with a twist. So, like, she used to make apricot jam, and I make it with apricot and lavender. Or instead of strawberry, I do strawberry with pink peppercorn and mint."

She reminded Cheryl of some girls she'd gone to high school with who were super sweet but came across as flighty because they thought boys liked that. But there were no boys here, so Cheryl assumed she was just genuinely deeply nice.

"Those sound delicious," Cheryl said, trying to be encouraging. But peppercorn? In jam? "Have you found many outlets to sell them here in town?"

"Mostly online. Most people said what you did, that they already have a jam supplier."

Cheryl nodded. There were plenty of people in these parts who made jam in more traditional flavors that she thought would be an easier sell. But she needed to find a way to see what this girl knew about the tainted jam, so she continued.

"Well, it turns out I may be looking for a new supplier."

"Really?" Bridget brightened noticeably.

"It turns out there have been some problems with the jam I usually buy recently," Cheryl said, watching her carefully. "Do you know Naomi Miller?"

Bridget nodded. "She is so sweet. My husband has been doing some computer work out at their place, and I've gotten to chat with Naomi some. I just adore her." She pulled down a basket of assorted teas, and Cheryl selected a peppermint blend. Bridget pushed a mug toward her.

"She's wonderful," Cheryl agreed, unwrapping the tea bag. "And we have been stocking her jam for years now, even before I started at the Swiss Miss. But somehow rat poison ended up in her last batch of jam, and several people have gone to the hospital and nearly died because of it."

"What?" Bridget's hand flew to her mouth. "Oh my goodness." Cheryl tried to gauge her reaction. She looked genuinely shocked. Like someone had just kicked a puppy.

"You hadn't heard about this? It's been in the newspapers."

Bridget shook her head. "I haven't read the paper. And I don't get into town much. But that's just awful. Are they going to be okay?"

"It looks like it." Cheryl continued to watch her. "Hopefully no new cases occur."

The teakettle began to whistle, and Bridget used a pot holder to pour the hot water over the tea bags.

"Are the people going to be all right?"

She didn't detect any traces of guilt in Bridget. More like confusion.

She nodded. "Yes, it looks like they will be fine because they got medical treatment right away."

After meeting her, it was hard to imagine this girl hurting a spider, let alone a human. But then, she'd been a long shot for the poisoner anyway.

"No kidding. Yikes. That's so terrible."

"Yes, well." Cheryl tried to smile. "Obviously we've had to pull Naomi's jams from the shelves. So now it seems like I may have some shelf space to give your jam a shot."

Cheryl mostly meant it. She'd said it partly to gauge Bridget's reaction, but it was also true. She did have shelf space to fill. And judging by what she'd seen so far, this girl could use the money. What would it hurt to buy a few dozen jars of her jam and give it a shot?

"Really?" She practically squealed. "Oh, that would be wonderful. Thank you so much! What flavors do you want? Oh, I have a new one, cranberry and sage, that is just wonderful."

"Maybe three of each flavor to start," Cheryl said. "And we'll see what sells the best."

"Oh my goodness. You totally made my day." Bridget clasped her hands and jumped up and down. "I'll go get the jars right now." And with that, she turned, yanked open a door, and flew down the stairs that Cheryl assumed led to the basement.

Cheryl picked up her tea and looked around the kitchen. On the refrigerator there were pictures of a little boy and a girl, niece and nephew, she assumed. Hanging over the small dinged-up wooden table was a framed version of Joshua 24:15 done in beautiful calligraphy—"As for me and my household, we will serve the Lord."

A few minutes later, Bridget came back into the kitchen carrying a cardboard box full of jam. She set it on the counter, and they briefly discussed cost and payment.

"Wonderful." Cheryl reached into the box and pulled out one jar of blood orange and rosemary. It was a beautiful, glistening deep red. It would look nice on the shelf, even if she never sold a jar of it.

Cheryl finished her tea as they chatted, and then she took the box of jam out to the car and headed back to town. She'd stayed a bit longer than she intended, and the sun was now hanging low in the sky. Yikes. She'd spent almost no time in the shop these past few days. She needed to get back.

As she drove back to town, she thought over the encounter and the girl. Once again she was stymied. Bridget was so far the only suspect who had a motive. She might have wanted to clear Naomi's jam off the shelves to make room for her own jam. But she was the only one who didn't have the opportunity. And…Cheryl didn't want to think anything mean, but she wasn't sure Bridget was crafty enough to plot out such an elaborate scheme. She really seemed like just a genuinely nice person with a bubbly personality.

She thought about the small, drafty little house, with the leaking roof and the pellet stove that didn't stand a chance. She and her husband were not living on a lot, she was pretty sure. But they were also young and had big dreams. In her time in Sugarcreek, she'd met a few people like Bridget who moved to the country for a simpler life, and some made it longer than others. She hoped they would make it.

She was lost in her thoughts when she was startled by her phone ringing. Keeping one hand on the wheel, she used the other to dig it out of her purse. It was the Miller house. Someone was calling her from the phone shanty out by the road.

"Hello?"

"Cheryl?" It was Levi.

"Hi, Levi." As much as she loved hearing the sound of his voice, her stomach clenched. Levi rarely called and certainly didn't call just to chat. "What's going on?"

"I wanted to let you know. The police were just here. They arrested Maam."

CHAPTER FIFTEEN

Cheryl drove directly to the Miller farm and picked up Levi and Seth and headed to the police station. She'd managed to get a few details from them before they left the house, but not many. All she knew was that Chief Twitchell and another officer had come in their police car and taken Naomi away.

"Did they say what evidence they had against her?" Cheryl asked.

Levi shook his head. "I do not think so," Seth answered.

"Did they read her her Miranda rights?"

Both men stared at her blankly. Oh, right. They hadn't grown up watching this element in every cop show in existence. "'You have the right to remain silent, you have the right to an attorney,' stuff like that?"

"I do not remember." Seth shook his head. "It all happened so fast, and we did not understand what was going on."

She nodded. It must have been scary and confusing for them. But mostly Cheryl was infuriated. How could Chief Twitchell go and arrest Naomi? He *knew* she hadn't done it. He couldn't possibly think... She needed to save her anger for later. Right now she needed to find out what had happened.

"What did he say when he came in? Did he ask questions at first, or did he just, you know, put her in handcuffs and lead her out?"

She glanced at Levi in the rearview mirror. His eyes were cast down at his lap. His jaw was clenched. He didn't say anything. Cheryl felt herself getting frustrated with him. How could she help if he didn't tell her what had happened? Why was he being like this?

"He did not ask questions," Seth finally said. "He came to arrest her, and arrest her he did."

Cheryl had more questions about how it had all gone down, but she was pulling up in front of the police station, so she set them aside for now. She'd go in and find out what was going on.

She parked and the Amish men climbed out of her car, and Cheryl scurried after them. Seth led the way into the front room of the police station.

"Hi, Cheryl. Levi. Seth." Delores saw the small party enter the station and gave a sympathetic smile. She picked up her phone. "She's in the back. Let me tell Chief Twitchell you're here."

A few minutes later, Officer Ortega escorted them back to the room at the rear of the station with a small holding cell. This gave Cheryl hope. She hadn't been moved to the Tuscarawas County Jail in New Philadelphia; she was being held in this small cell that was only used for short-term detainments.

"Only two visitors at a time," Officer Ortega said tonelessly. Cheryl had never heard such a rule before, but she looked at Seth and Levi and she immediately hung back.

"Thank you, Cheryl," Seth said, and he followed the police officer into the room. There was a small bench pressed up against the wall outside the room, and Cheryl assumed she was supposed to wait there, but she knew she was too keyed up to sit still. Instead, she started down the hallway and headed straight for Chief Twitchell's office.

"Chief Twitchell." She didn't even knock, just barged right in.

He was on the phone, but when he saw Cheryl and how angry she was, he said, "I'll have to call you back," and hung up the phone.

"You *arrested* Naomi?" Cheryl realized she was almost shouting, but she didn't care.

"Now, first of all, calm down, Cheryl."

Usually she found his Southern accent charming, but right now it was just infuriating.

"I can't believe you arrested her. For what? On what grounds?"

"Cheryl, take a deep breath."

Telling an angry person to calm down was probably the least helpful thing you could do, Cheryl thought. But she realized she needed to get herself under control if she wanted him to talk to her, so she took a moment to take a deep breath, and then, in her most calm voice, continued.

"Please tell me why my sweet Amish friend is behind bars."

He hesitated for a moment.

Cheryl continued. "You don't really believe she poisoned her jam, do you?"

"Cheryl, I…"

"Because you know as well as I do that she did nothing of the sort. So can you explain to me why she's locked up?"

He didn't say anything for a moment. And then, uncertainly, he said, "My hands are tied. I'm gettin' a lot of pressure from my superiors at the state level to make an arrest. Without anyone to pin it on, I had to arrest Naomi. It's an open-and-shut case."

Cheryl understood what he was saying. The state senator wanted someone to hold responsible for his wife's illness, and he was using his influence to make sure it happened. Never mind if the person arrested hadn't actually committed the crime.

"What about Stan McCullough?"

He shook his head. "We talked to him. He says he didn't do it."

"Naomi says the same thing. And *she's* telling the truth."

"There is no proof, Cheryl. Nothin' to link him to the crime."

"Nothing that will hold up in court, you mean."

"That too." He sighed.

"That is the worst excuse for a . . . "

"There is nothin' I could have done, Cheryl."

Cheryl didn't believe that for a second. There were plenty of things he could have done, and standing up for the truth was just the start. But she knew cursing him out wasn't going to get her anywhere, so she tried to keep her anger in check. For now, she had to focus on getting him to work with her.

"You and I both know she didn't do it," Cheryl said. "So how are we going to get her out?"

"Unfortunately, the judge who handles cases like these over at the courthouse is away for the next few days."

"What?"

"Yeah. In the Bahamas. Where I wish I was right now."

Cheryl couldn't believe he was talking about his vacation wishes after what he'd just told her.

"So what does that mean, that the judge is away?"

"I'm afraid it means bail can't be set."

"So, what? She's just going to sit here in this cell all weekend until the judge gets back from her vacation?"

"Well…" He shifted in his chair. "Not exactly. She'll be transferred to the county jail until her bail hearing can be arranged."

At this news, Cheryl just about lost it. Only the admonition in Scripture to not let any unwholesome talk come out of her mouth kept her from letting loose a string of expletives that would be heard all the way over at the county jail.

"I'm sorry, Cheryl. Truly I am. I will explain to her family what's happenin', and…"

"Andy Glick and Martha Esch."

"Excuse me?"

"Those are the names of the Amish people who might have poisoned the jam." Cheryl knew Naomi hadn't wanted to involve the other members of her community, but Cheryl wasn't going to let Naomi just sit here rotting in jail while the real culprit went free. If it meant ratting out the potential suspects to get her friend free, it was worth it. "Martha is four years old. She is Naomi's cousin's daughter who stopped by the day they made the jam. She might have mixed up rat poison with the pectin."

He had started scribbling hurriedly but looked up. "The what?"

"Pectin. You use it to make jam. Andy Glick is Eli's friend. He likes to play practical jokes. This is apparently the kind of thing he would have found funny."

The police chief stopped scribbling and looked up at Cheryl.

"Thank you."

"Now can Naomi go?"

He shook his head. "I appreciate the names, but I'm afraid I can't release her until the bail hearing on Monday."

"Are you serious?"

He nodded.

Cheryl pushed herself up. "In that case, you can expect to be hearing from my lawyer shortly."

"You have a lawyer?"

"I will soon." And with that, Cheryl turned and walked out the door.

Chapter Sixteen

Cheryl spent a bit of time with Naomi, who was in good spirits, considering the fact that she sat behind bars for a crime she hadn't committed. Cheryl was relieved to see she was still wearing her Amish dress instead of some prison jumpsuit. Cheryl hoped they would let her keep her dress at the prison in New Philadelphia. Being forced to wear English convict's clothes would be the worst indignity she could think of for her Amish friend.

"Is there anything you need?" Cheryl asked.

Her sweet friend shook her head. "I do not need anything. But please make sure my family is all right. I do not mind being in here as long as I know my family is well taken care of."

"Of course." Cheryl held her friend's hand through the bars. How like Naomi to worry about other people, even in this predicament.

Then Levi and Seth came in again to say good-bye before they had to leave. Naomi was about to be transferred to the county jail, and none of them wanted to stay to see her loaded into the back of a police car.

The drive back to the farm was quiet and tense. Cheryl tried several times to get Levi to talk to her, but his answers always came in short, simple sentences that ended the conversation. Cheryl noticed that his knuckles were white where he clenched the door handle.

They said good-bye, and they promised to let her know if they heard any news. Cheryl also promised to try to find a good lawyer to represent Naomi, and Seth thanked her. She knew Naomi would be assigned a DA if no lawyer took the case, but based on what Cheryl had heard, Naomi would be better off with a lawyer paid to be on their side. As Cheryl drove home in the darkening twilight, she prayed for Naomi, for the whole Miller family, and that God would bring the truth to light quickly.

Once she got inside, she warmed up some leftover baked ziti, and then she tried to figure out who to hire as a lawyer. She had a feeling she should get a recommendation from a friend.

Beau nuzzled her hand, begging to be petted. She stroked his head absently.

Well . . . She thought for a moment. Her friend Jessica Stockton's husband Jeff worked in the county recorder's office over in New Philadelphia. Maybe he would have interacted with someone who might be able to help. Cheryl called Jessica and explained the situation, and Jessica promised to pass the message along to Jeff and try to get back to her with some names as soon as possible.

Cheryl was too keyed up to go to sleep, but she didn't know what else to do, so she sat down in front of her computer and tried to find out everything she could about her suspects.

She'd already researched Stan McCullough thoroughly, and no matter how many pages she scrolled through, she didn't find out any more about him. Googling Martha Esch was a bust, and she found an Instagram account for Andy Glick, but all it contained were pictures of himself making funny faces.

Then she tried searching for the name Bridget Marshall again. The first thing that came up was a Facebook page, just as it had before. Cheryl scrolled through the posts, seeing photo after photo of a stylized, idealized life. The pictures showed Bridget gazing out over the fields, raking up golden leaves, holding up fresh produce. "I love farming!" one post boasted, and another showed mason jars of freshly made jam lined up along the counter. "Nothing beats homemade," the caption read. A picture of the ground littered with fallen, rotting apples under an arching tree was labeled #farmerfail.

Cheryl tried to reconcile the beautiful, simple life she saw on screen with the frozen, lonely life she'd witnessed that day. There was nothing on the site that showed the leaking ceiling, or the way the pellet stove had turned the linoleum in the kitchen brown, or how they could only afford one car so Bridget was stuck alone in a house in the middle of nowhere most of the time. Like most people, Bridget no doubt tried to make herself look as good as possible online. But was this idealized version of her life even close to reality? Was this how Bridget truly saw the world—or how she wanted the world to see her?

Cheryl scrolled down her profile and saw photos of her wedding to Carter that past summer. She'd made a beautiful bride, and Carter was handsome, with a chiseled chin and high cheekbones. Before that were shots from their college graduation in May, and various parties and events before that. Cheryl saw that she was originally from a suburb of Cincinnati and that she had two sisters. Cheryl kept scrolling but found herself growing frustrated. There was nothing useful here. She'd been hoping for some sort of clue, but all she was finding was more evidence of a carefully curated online presence.

She clicked back to the main search page and found her Etsy site. Etsy was the Web site where people sold handmade crafts and art, and Cheryl opened the page to see a nicely designed site. SweetBlossom Designs was the name of her shop, and at the bottom of the page, there was a picture of Bridget, her brown hair curling prettily around her face, as well as a link to a page with more information about her. Cheryl clicked on that and read that Bridget's love of all things homemade had been born from watching her grandmother knit, can, cook, and make beautiful handmade pieces of art. Cheryl looked back at the page and saw the letter-pressed and calligraphied cards and the hand-knit scarves and sweaters. Actually, that one sweater was kind of cute…

No. Cheryl forced herself not to get distracted by things she didn't need.

Well, Bridget seemed to be good enough at what she did, and her prices were reasonable, but Cheryl was no closer to finding out if she'd poisoned the jam or not. Still, she printed out the page just in case, and she tucked it into her purse with her other notes.

Finally, Cheryl pushed herself back. She wasn't getting anywhere. She was exhausted, but she still didn't feel like she could fall asleep. She forced herself to take a shower, climb under the covers, and close her eyes. She prayed for Naomi. She prayed for Levi, that he would stop shutting her out. She prayed for wisdom and guidance as she sought the truth. She prayed for Aunt Mitzi and for all the people she was ministering to in Papua New Guinea. And as the peace of God came over her, finally, eventually, Cheryl drifted off to sleep.

CHAPTER SEVENTEEN

The next morning, Cheryl looked online and saw that the headline in the paper was Amish Woman Arrested for Poisoning Jam. Cheryl groaned. Then she clicked over to her e-mail and checked her messages as she ate breakfast, and she was thrilled to see that Jeff Stockton had written to her, recommending the name of a lawyer he knew who had a lot of experience working on criminal cases like the one she was describing. The words struck her. Naomi was charged with a criminal case.

Well, she would just have to prove that her friend was not a criminal, and hopefully this lawyer would help. She called the number for Anthony Fordham, Attorney at Law, at his office in New Philadelphia. He didn't pick up—Cheryl realized that it was barely past 8:00 a.m., which probably explained it—and she left a message asking him to please call her back. She didn't have any idea how much his services would cost, but she would help cover them if needed, especially since the Miller family would be losing out on the income from selling jam.

Then she pushed her way up and made her way to the shop. She went through the motions of opening up the store—lighting the wood-burning stove, booting up the computer, opening the register—but she was distracted the whole time, thinking about poor Naomi and wondering how she'd made out during her night in the jail. But there was no way to call her and ask. She lugged the box of Bridget's jam in from her car and set it on the shelf where Naomi's jam used to be. It looked so out of place there—the wrong size jar, the wrong label, the wrong flavors. But at least she had jam on the shelves.

Cheryl decided she should probably taste the jam, in case anyone asked about it. She looked through the flavors on the shelf and settled on cranberry with sage. She found a package of saltines in the back room and opened the jar with a satisfying pop. She used a plastic knife to spread the jam on a cracker and took a bite. It was tart but sweet somehow, and the sage added an earthy fresh flavor that was actually quite delicious. Cheryl finished the cracker and spread the jam on another one. Actually, this was really good. She ate several more crackers spread with jam and then forced herself to stop. If she could convince people to try this stuff, they would love it. But she knew crazy flavors like this were going to be a tough sell.

Cheryl called the number for Anthony Fordham, the lawyer Jeff had recommended again, and this time she got ahold of his secretary, who said she could squeeze Cheryl in at four o'clock that afternoon. Cheryl had been hoping she could talk to him sooner, and the thought of Naomi sitting in that jail all day bothered her, but she wasn't sure what else to do. She booked the appointment and said she'd be there.

After Lydia and Esther came in, there were a few customers, but then the shop was quiet again. Cheryl was surprised to see

Esther, and the girl's face was pale and her eyes were red. Cheryl offered that she could go home, but Esther wanted to stay. She said she needed something to keep her mind off of the mess at home. Cheryl pumped Esther for information about Naomi, but she didn't seem to have any new information Cheryl didn't already have.

Then, in what seemed like an effort to brighten the mood, Esther said, "I think you have created a monster, Cheryl."

"What do you mean?"

"Eli could hardly be dragged away from those skis you brought over to finish his chores this morning."

Cheryl smiled. "I'm glad he likes them." She thought back to that night she'd tried to teach them both. "Has Levi tried his on again?"

"Oh yes. Eli was making such a big deal out of it that Levi put them on again, only he did not do so well."

"No?" Cheryl felt bad that she smiled.

Esther shook her head. "No. He fell a few times, and then he tossed the skis and called them *lecherich*."

"Lecherich?"

"Ridiculous," Lydia said, looking up from the shelf she was dusting from nearby.

Cheryl had to laugh a bit at that. "I wish I could have seen that."

"Why?" Esther looked genuinely confused.

"Because Levi is so even-tempered. It's hard to imagine him losing his cool."

Esther and Lydia looked at one another. Then Esther said, slowly, "He is even-tempered for the most part. You are right about that. But when he gets mad, he really can throw a tantrum."

"Really?" Even as she said it, though, Cheryl thought about what she'd seen in the past few days. Hadn't she seen him growing sullen and then angry and hard to reach? She hadn't seen him lose his temper in a dramatic way—that was more Cheryl's style—but she could understand what Esther was saying now in a way she wouldn't have been able to just a week ago. And it was unsettling. "I guess you're right."

"He has gotten better as he has gotten older," Esther added, no doubt trying to be helpful. But now that she was thinking about it, Cheryl couldn't stop thinking about Levi. Was he okay? Surely what was going on with Naomi had contributed to his temper flaring this morning. Could Cheryl help? Had she made it worse?

Soon Cheryl's stomach was rumbling, and she could tell the Amish girls were hungry too. Since the shop was dead, Esther volunteered to go to Yoder's Corner and pick up sausage and rolls for them all. Cheryl didn't indulge in sausage very often, but on a cold winter Friday, it seemed like the best thing she could think of. Even better that she didn't have to go outside to get it.

"She just wants to talk to Rosella about the Singing tomorrow," Lydia said with a wink as soon as Esther was gone.

"She will still go even with what's going on with her mom?"

"I suppose."

Well, good for her. The girl works too hard. Let her have some fun.

While Cheryl waited for the sausage to arrive, she sat down at the counter. She pulled out her list of suspects and her notes and peered at it one more time, willing something new to jump out at her.

"Andy Glick?" Lydia came around the counter and reached for a dustpan. "What has he done now? He does not have anything to do with the jam, does he?"

Cheryl wondered for a moment if she should remind Lydia that it wasn't polite to read over someone's shoulder, but she didn't. Instead, she turned to the girl and decided what she could tell her about him.

"I don't know," Cheryl said. "Do you think he could have?"

Lydia set the dustpan down on the counter. "I do not think so."

"No?" Cheryl looked at her. "A lot of other people seem to think he might have thought it was funny."

Lydia hesitated. "Yes, I can see why they think that. He has a reputation for being a funny guy, someone who is always playing practical jokes. But I do not know. We hung out a few times last year..." Cheryl wondered if Lydia was interested in him, but Lydia seemed to read her thoughts and shook her head. "Just talking after Sunday service and such. I think he is interested in Marianna Coblentz. But he doesn't have very many people who listen and treat him like an adult. I got the sense that he used to be that guy. Now he has grown up and does not want to be like that anymore, but no one takes him seriously because they think of him as this silly kid. So he behaves in his jokey way to make people happy. It is an act that he feels like has to keep up, but it is no longer what he wants to be. And he says he hasn't done any practical jokes in almost a year, but no one has really noticed because all they see is what they want to see in him."

Well, this was a new perspective. "He's said that?"

"More or less. I think that is why he is struggling with whether to join the church. Everyone thinks it is just because he likes cars and cell phones, and it is true that he does, but he also is not sure the community is ever going to see him for who he really is."

This was interesting. If Lydia was right, it was much easier to believe that he had been telling the truth about having nothing to do with the jam.

But it still didn't prove anything, Cheryl thought. And that was the rub. She couldn't get her best friend free from jail unless she could find some way to prove who really had committed the crime. But in any case, Lydia had given her a perspective that she hadn't heard from anyone else yet. Cheryl decided to see what else she could tell her.

"Do you know Martha Esch?" Cheryl asked.

Lydia pursed her lips together and thought for a moment. "Sylvia's daughter?"

"Exactly."

"You think she might have poisoned the jam?"

"Not on purpose. But there's a chance she might have had something to do with it."

Lydia shrugged. "I do not know. She is just a child. It is hard to say. She seems sweet, but I don't really interact with her much." She thought for a moment. "Her maam has always seemed pretty sharp to me. She always seems to know what her children are doing, not like some people who never seem to know where their children are. It is hard for me to imagine her letting Martha get far enough away to make a mistake like that. But I do not know." She glanced over at Cheryl's list. "Who else you got?"

Lydia had joined the church and renounced the English ways she'd adopted during *rumspringa*, but Cheryl loved that sometimes she still caught a glimpse of the Lydia she had first met, if only in speech.

"An appliance repairman named Stan McCullough." Cheryl pointed to the name in her notes.

"Do not know him," Lydia said. "Anyone else?"

"I was looking into this girl, Bridget Marshall," Cheryl said, shuffling to the pages she'd printed out from her Etsy shop. "That's her jam on the shelf."

Lydia made a face that showed what she thought of that jam. "I do not know her. What do you know about her?" she asked.

"Not a lot." Cheryl shuffled to the page with her photo. "This is her."

"Oh." Lydia paused and looked down at the picture. "Wait, this is Bridget?"

"Yes. Why?" Cheryl sat up a bit straighter. "Do you know her after all?"

Lydia squinted at the picture and then shook her head. "I do not know her, but I recognize her. She came in here on Saturday."

"Wait, what?" Cheryl stammered. "Like, here, as in, she was in the Swiss Miss?"

Lydia continued to look at the picture and nodded. "Yes, I am sure it was her. You were grabbing lunch and Esther had not come in yet, and I went up to her and asked her if she needed help."

"What did she say?"

"She said no," Lydia said. "So I left her alone. But I watched her a bit. Something about her seemed off."

"Off?"

"Like, she seemed annoyed that I talked to her. And she was moving quickly, like she was nervous. I do not know. There was something about her that made me pay attention."

"And did you see anything?"

"No." Lydia shook her head, and the strings on her kapp swung. "She didn't buy anything, just looked around a bit and walked out."

Saturday. The poisoned jam had been sold on Saturday. Was there any way... Cheryl tried to picture the scene.

"Where did you talk to her?"

"She was over there." Lydia swallowed hard as if she realized what she was about to say. "Over by the shelf of jams."

This was too much of a coincidence to be purely accidental. Months after Cheryl had told her she couldn't stock her jams, she showed up here by the jam section on the same day a jar of poisoned jam was sold? Cheryl still didn't understand a lot of things about what could have happened, but she knew that this was too clear of a link to be ignored.

"What was she wearing? Did she have a bag with her?"

"I do not remember what she was wearing. But she did have a bag. It was a large quilted thing. I remember thinking it looked heavy."

"Like it could have been full?"

Lydia nodded. "Full of jam."

Was that it? Had she come in here with jars of the tainted jam and planted them on the shelf?

Cheryl knew she was jumping to some pretty big conclusions here. And she had no idea how the poison would have gotten into the jam because Bridget was definitively not there on the day the jam was canned and the jars had been sold sealed.

But again, her showing up here—and acting strangely and looking around without buying anything—on the day the tainted jam was sold seemed more than a little unlikely. Had the girl also visited the Honey Bee that day? And Yoder's Corner?

It seemed too crazy to be believable. What would her motive have been? To ruin the reputation of the most popular jam supplier so businesses would start stocking her jams instead? Cheryl had already come up with and dismissed that motive as too far-out.

But then—Cheryl looked over to the shelf of jam she'd stocked just this morning—that's what had happened, wasn't it? Naomi's jam had been pulled from the shelves, and Bridget's jam was there instead.

But poison? Would even a girl driven by the desperate need to bring in income have resorted to poisoning her rival's jam? It seemed far too outlandish to even consider. Someone could have very easily died. It would have taken a coldhearted brute to have attempted to eliminate the competition by eliminating her customers. And Bridget was anything but coldhearted. She was sweet and warm and friendly.

Cheryl had a hunch she was on to something, but right now all it was was wild speculation. She needed to find answers somehow. She sat back and thought. If Bridget had brought in jam that she'd messed with in some way, what were the chances she'd only brought in one jar? Could she have somehow tainted a number of jars? And if so, could any of the others be here still?

Cheryl pushed herself up and went into the back room, where she'd left the box of jam she'd pulled from the shelf. She hefted it up and carried it back out to the counter and set it down. She pulled one jar of strawberry from the box and stared at it.

"What are you looking for?" Lydia asked.

"I'm not sure," Cheryl admitted. So far all the people who had gotten sick had eaten strawberry jam, so she focused on that now. She studied the handwritten label carefully. It was done in Naomi's looping script by her fine-nibbed pen. The date on this batch was the same as the date from the tainted batch. It looked just like it should.

Cheryl set that jar aside and looked at the next one in the box. It was also from the same batch, according to the date. But... Cheryl squinted at the label. Was she imagining this, or was there really a slight difference in the handwriting on this one? She pulled back and compared this jar to the other.

No, she wasn't imagining it. The way the tail on the *y* was looped was slightly thinner on this second jar. And the *t* was crossed with a less bold stroke as well. And... She looked back and forth. There were probably a dozen small differences in the handwriting between the two jars.

But was this just normal variation in how Naomi had printed? Cheryl's handwriting wasn't exactly the same every time she wrote. She pulled a third jar out of the box and studied it. The *y* matched the first jar, as did the *t*. The handwriting was very similar to the second jar, but not exactly the same. However, it was pretty much exactly the same as the first jar. Cheryl pulled out a few other jars to compare and came to the same conclusion.

"What is it?" Lydia asked.

Just then the door blew open and Esther came in, her cheeks pink, holding a bag of takeout from Yoder's Corner. She took off her coat and made her way down the aisle. Cheryl's stomach rumbled when she smelled the sausage.

"What is going on?" Esther asked. She set the bag down and started unpacking foil-wrapped plastic containers.

Cheryl held up the second jar of jam, the one that looked ever so slightly off to Cheryl. "Is this your mother's handwriting?" she asked.

Esther set a plastic container in front of Lydia and leaned in and took a look.

"I think so," Esther said. "Why? It is her jam. Why would it not be?"

"How about this one?" Cheryl held up the first jar.

"*Hmm.*" Esther set a foil-wrapped sausage and a roll in front of Cheryl. "You know, it looks a little different from the other jar. But I think this one belongs to my maam."

"You're sure?"

"I am not sure," Esther said. "But I think so. This label"—she pointed to the second jar—"does not look like it was written by my maam."

"I think so too," Cheryl said. "It's close, but it's not quite right."

Esther nodded. "But if that is the case, who wrote this label? And why?"

Cheryl felt a slow smile creep across her face. She remembered something Lydia had told her and something she'd seen the previous day.

"I have a suspicion I know who it was."

CHAPTER EIGHTEEN

It was nearly time for Esther's shift to end, and it was a few hours earlier than she'd normally close up the shop, but the week had been so quiet Cheryl didn't think she'd be losing too many sales if she closed a bit early tonight. Besides, this way she'd have time to check out her ideas at the farm before she had to head over to her appointment with the lawyer.

So after they finished closing out the register, they cleaned up the shop and took out the trash, and then Cheryl turned off the lights and locked the door. They waved good-bye to Lydia, and then she and Esther climbed into her car.

Clouds were gathering in the west, and the air felt a bit warmer, but it smelled like snow. A storm was gathering on the horizon, but for now it was a smooth, easy drive.

Soon they pulled up in front of the house, and Cheryl followed Esther inside. The kitchen was quiet, and the house somehow felt hollow. Naomi's absence felt like an actual presence somehow. They found Elizabeth in the living room, working on sewing, and she informed them that Seth was at the jail visiting Naomi, Levi was out in the barn, and Eli was out in the yard practicing on the skis.

"With all that is going on, Eli is out there skiing?" Esther said, her voice rising.

Elizabeth shrugged. "I suppose it is his way of dealing with it."

"It would be nice if he could 'deal with it' by doing something productive, like the rest of us."

"Perhaps it feels productive to him."

Esther mumbled something under her breath in Dutch, and then she said in English, "Cheryl thinks she knows who really poisoned the jam."

Elizabeth gasped. "Wirklich?"

Cheryl looked blankly at her, and Elizabeth continued, "Really?"

"I wouldn't say that," Cheryl said quickly. No need to get anyone's hopes up until they knew more. "But I do have a suspicion. I was hoping I could take a look at your mother's canning supplies downstairs."

"Who is it?"

Cheryl hesitated. All signs pointed to Bridget, but she didn't want to slander the girl if she was wrong. She was pretty sure that holding back was what an Amish person would do.

"I'll tell you when I know for sure," she said, and Elizabeth nodded. Cheryl knew holding one's tongue was a virtue they all tried to practice. "For now, can I see the basement?"

"Of course." Elizabeth pushed herself up, and she led the way, with Esther and Cheryl following behind. They went through the kitchen toward the door that led to the basement. Cheryl had been in this basement many times, and though it was nice as far as basements go—kept clean and tidy—it was still damp and, with the absence of overhead lights, very dark. Pale winter light streamed in through the transom windows high on the walls, but it was still hard to see. Cheryl pulled out her phone and turned on the flashlight feature as they descended the wooden stairs. Against the wall closest to the stairs sat the boxy white propane-powered freezer Stan McCullough had been here to repair. On the opposite wall were various household items—holiday items as well as boxes of baby clothes and blankets. All the boxes were meticulously labeled and stacked neatly. At the end of these shelves was a section that held cans of paint, extra bottles of kerosene, and various boxes that looked forbidding.

"Is the rat poison kept over here?" Cheryl asked, and Esther nodded, showing her the box marked with a skull and crossbones. It was on a low enough shelf that Martha theoretically could have reached it. It probably should have been kept on a higher shelf, but she supposed that since there weren't small children in the household, they hadn't thought about that.

"Maam's canning supplies are over here, by her jam," Elizabeth said, pointing toward a section of shelves on the wall behind the stairs. Cheryl had seen the rows and rows of jams, preserves, and canned vegetables, picked fresh from her garden. There was enough food down here to feed the family for months, and Cheryl knew from experience that Naomi's fruits and vegetables, canned from produce grown right here on the farm, were fresh and healthy and delicious. At the end of the row were boxes of empty jars as well as a rubber bin full of supplies. A box of pectin sat open on a low shelf.

She looked from the small box of pectin to the rat poison on the other side of the basement. It was hard to imagine how even a four-year-old would confuse the two. It just didn't seem likely, now that she'd seen it, that Martha had been looking for the ingredients for making jam among the paint cans and fertilizers. Even if she couldn't read, and even though it was dark in here, the child would know to look among the other canning supplies, or at the very least, near the jars. Cheryl felt better about crossing poor little Martha off her list.

"Where does your mother keep the labels she uses on her jars?" Cheryl asked.

"In that box," Esther said, indicating the plastic box of supplies. "Would you like to look?"

"Yes, please," Cheryl said. Elizabeth pulled the box off the shelf, and they all trooped back up the stairs to examine it with better light. Esther popped the lid off. Inside were extra jar lids, neat stacks of cheesecloth, blocks of wax, and various tools Cheryl didn't recognize.

"What is this?" Cheryl asked, holding up a metal utensil with handles on one end and rubberized grips on the other.

"That is a jar lifter," Elizabeth said. "For taking jars out of the hot water."

"Ah." Who knew things like this even existed?

Finally, Cheryl found what she was looking for: packages of the off-white labels Naomi used to label her jars, as well as a pack of the nibbed pens she always used.

"Do you happen to know the last time your mother made jam?" Cheryl asked, examining the packages of labels. One was open, and there were two spare packages. They were press-and-stick, like a fancier version of mailing labels you would get from an office supply store. It felt so wrong to be asking Naomi's daughters instead of Naomi herself. She sure hoped they could find answers and free her friend soon.

"I do not think she has made any since that day," Esther said, looking at her sister. Elizabeth nodded.

"Would you be able to tell if some of her labels were missing?" Cheryl tried to guess how many were gone from the open package.

"I do not know," Esther said. "I am not sure how many Maam used."

"What about the pens?"

Both girls shook their heads. "It looks like there are about three missing from the package," Esther added, "but I could not know how many Maam has used."

Cheryl had expected as much. Still, she had seen one thing for sure: it was possible that someone could have taken labels and a pen to mimic Naomi's labels if they knew where to look.

"Can you tell me the last time Bridget Marshall was here?" Cheryl asked.

Elizabeth gasped. "You think it was Bridget?"

Esther nodded smugly, pleased to have been in on the secret.

"I don't know," Cheryl reiterated. "I'm just trying to figure out if it is possible."

"I said I thought she had come over last week while I was at work, but I could not be sure," Esther said.

"*Ja*, that is right," Elizabeth said. "I believe it was last Monday. That was a day when her husband had been scheduled to come set up the wireless network. He had finally gotten some part he needed..."

"A router," Esther said, pride on her face.

"A router," Elizabeth continued. "And she came in and chatted with Maam while she was baking a pie to take to Kathryn Beachy, who had pneumonia."

Cheryl wasn't sure that a pie was exactly what someone with pneumonia needed, but that was beside the point. She loved that pie was the Amish answer to everything.

"Did Bridget ever go into the basement that day?"

Elizabeth thought for a moment, putting her hand under her chin. The gesture reminded Cheryl so much of Naomi it almost hurt.

"You know, I think she did," Elizabeth said. "She said she was looking into putting up a canning shelf at her home, and she wanted to check out ours."

"Did anyone go down to the basement with her?"

"I do not think so. I was rolling out the crust, and Maam was stirring the custard as it thickened," Elizabeth said. Cheryl assumed in their world this explained why Naomi couldn't have gone to the basement with Bridget, but she'd never made custard, so she wasn't sure. In any case, Bridget had gone to the basement alone. Which meant that Cheryl's theory was lining up.

They had just established a timeline that made it possible for Bridget to have taken leftover labels and jars and relabeled them. But that still left the problem of why she'd done so, as well as how she got the poison inside the sealed jars. Surely they would have noticed if there had been cracks or fissures in the jars...

"It is hard to imagine Bridget doing something like this," Elizabeth said. "Why would she do it? She seems so nice. She sat here and drank tea and chatted about her nieces and nephews."

"And how?" Esther added. "I still do not understand that."

"That's what I can't get my head around," Cheryl said. "Let me make sure I've got this straight. There's no possible way the jars could have been opened and resealed?"

"That's not exactly right," Elizabeth said. "You could open a jar of jam and add something to it, but that would break the seal. If you want to seal it again, you would need to reprocess the jar."

"And that means?"

"Closing the lid tightly and boiling the jar in a large pot of water."

"But if you did that, the label would come off," Cheryl said.

Elizabeth nodded.

"But..." Esther's eyes lit up, and Cheryl saw that she understood what Cheryl was getting at. "But if you had another label on hand, and you could make your handwriting match that of the handwriting on the original label, no one would ever know that the jar had been opened."

"And Bridget knows calligraphy," Cheryl added. "She does it well enough that she sells her work online."

"Goodness." Esther scooted her chair closer to the table. "So she really could have been the one who did this thing."

"She *could* have," Cheryl agreed.

"It sounds like maybe she did," Esther said.

Cheryl didn't want to get too excited, but she had to agree.

Before she could change her mind, she pulled out her phone and placed a call to Chief Twitchell.

CHAPTER NINETEEN

Chief Twitchell wasn't in when Cheryl called. She left a message and asked him to call her back as soon as possible. It was an emergency, she told Delores, who promised to pass along the message. Before Cheryl went off to keep her appointment with the lawyer, she stopped by the barn to say hi to Levi.

"Hey there," she called as she pulled open the heavy barn door and stepped inside. The musty, woody smell of clean hay hit her. Weak sunlight filtered in, and it took a minute for her eyes to adjust. Then she spotted Levi over by the horses. He was bent over, mucking out stalls with a pitchfork and wheelbarrow.

"Hello, Cheryl," he called, straightening up. He rested the pitchfork on the ground, and a wide smile spread across his face. She walked toward him. "It is good to see you," he said.

Cheryl let out a breath she hadn't realized she'd been holding. He genuinely seemed pleased to see her. After the tension in the car the last time she'd seen him, she hadn't been sure if he would be happy to see her or not.

"I brought Esther home, and I was talking to her and Elizabeth for a bit, so I wanted to say hello."

"I am so glad you did."

She stopped a few feet from him. Her heart swelled. He was so handsome. Even in the dim light of the barn, his blond hair seemed to catch the sun, and his blue eyes were focused on her like he didn't want to look away.

"How is Spice?" she asked, indicating the mare that stood in the walkway at the end of the row while he cleaned out her stall.

"Spice is fine. But Ranger misses you."

Cheryl nodded and stepped around Levi to the next stall, where the sweet-tempered black horse Levi had given her for her birthday stood. She held out her hand, and he came forward and ducked his head, nudging it up under her hand. She stroked the smooth hair on his nose.

"I've missed you, boy," she said, running her hands along his head to the fine, silky mane. She needed to come out and see him more when she was out at the farm. And it wasn't exactly prime riding weather, but come spring, she couldn't wait to go riding.

"Oh, now I see why you are really here," Levi said. He was smiling.

"I came to see both of you," Cheryl insisted. She gave Ranger one last nuzzle, then dropped her hand and turned back to Levi. "But mostly you. How are you doing?"

He let out a mirthless laugh. "Oh, you know. About how you would expect, considering my maam is in jail for something she did not do." He gave her a sad smile, and then he picked up his pitchfork again. "Daed is over at the jail now. I hope he will have a good report."

He bent over and shoved the pitchfork into the pile of soiled straw in Spice's stall and scooped up a load. Cheryl loved to watch him work, to see how powerful his body was, how strong his daily tasks had made him. Lance had spent hours in the gym each day and still hadn't been this fit and strong.

"I am headed to New Philadelphia to talk to a lawyer after this. I am hopeful he'll be able to help us get her out."

Levi dropped the soiled straw into the wheelbarrow. "I hope so too."

She wanted to ask him how he was really doing, get him to open up and tell her his feelings. But she didn't know how to get underneath his shell. She knew he felt many things, but, like most Amish men, those feelings seemed to be buried deep.

"If there is any other way I can help, I want to," she said, moving closer to him.

He paused and looked at her and gave a hint of a smile, and then he said, "I know." Then he shoveled another load of straw.

Cheryl watched him work for a few moments, trying to figure out what else to say. But she couldn't think of how to get him to tell her what he was really feeling. She decided to change the subject.

"I hear Eli has been practicing on his skis a lot."

"Oh yes." He pitched another load of straw into the wheelbarrow. "He has been doing nothing but playing around in the yard."

"I was wondering if you wanted another lesson. Without him around, I could really work with you to help you feel more comfortable."

"That is all right." He kept moving, pitching loads of straw. Little clouds of dust went up every time he heaved a load into the barrow. "I do not think skiing is for me."

"You only tried it once. I don't think it's fair to say . . . "

"I did not enjoy it. I do not think it is for me."

There was a hardness, an anger in his voice that she'd never heard before.

"No one enjoys it at first, but once you get the hang of it, trust me, you'll love it." If she could just get him to give it a real shot, she was sure he'd love it.

"I said I do not want to do it." His voice still had that steely tenor, and he was not looking at her. "Eli may think it is fun, zipping around here on wooden sticks, skipping out on his work, but I do not. I do not like falling, and I do not see how this is supposed to be fun. Someone needs to keep this farm running. There is a reason Amish men do not do things like skiing. I will not talk more about it."

His words felt like a slap. Cheryl wasn't sure what to say. It wasn't like she was dragging him to a mountain and buying him a lift pass. She was just trying to share something she loved with the man she loved. But he was giving up before he'd even really started. Cheryl wanted to argue, but she also wanted to curl up and cry.

Instead, she turned to go. She did not know what else to do. She had never seen Levi like this, and she had no idea how to respond to him or how to change his mind.

"All right then," she said, forcing herself to keep her voice light. "I'd better go see that lawyer."

Levi nodded, but he kept his eyes on his work. A thousand emotions coursed through her. What was going on with Levi?

Was the situation with Naomi causing him to act uncharacteristically harsh, or was this the way he really was and she had never seen it? Was he frustrated at the situation or at her?

But the thought that kept turning over in her mind as she walked to her car was, did she really know Levi at all?

CHAPTER TWENTY

Cheryl drove to New Philadelphia to meet with the lawyer Jeff had recommended, Anthony Fordham, and the meeting went well. Seth, who had taken a van to New Philadelphia earlier that day, met her at the office, and they spoke with Anthony together. He agreed to take on the case and seemed certain he could help get Naomi cleared. He promised to start gathering information that evening.

When they got out of the meeting with the lawyer, Cheryl checked her phone and saw that Chief Twitchell hadn't called her back, so she called the police station again. Delores said that the police chief was out on a call but promised once again to pass on the message, and once again Cheryl reiterated that it was an emergency.

Cheryl drove Seth home but declined the invitation to come in. She didn't want to face Levi, and the house just felt empty without Naomi. Instead, she went home and ate a dinner of spaghetti and meatballs. Then she checked her phone—still no message from the police chief—and snuggled up with Beau on the couch and thought about what she was going to say to Twitchell when he called. She knew she had to get this right because he was already predisposed to not believe her. They had a suspect, Naomi, in custody. An open-and-shut case, he'd called it. She needed to be able to convince him that she knew who the real culprit was.

She thought it through. She'd tell the police that she'd been working under the assumption that the poison had to have been put into jars before they were sealed, but now she knew the jars could have been resealed. All she had to do was open them, sprinkle in the poison, and... What was the next step?

Cheryl had thought she'd had it right in her mind, but she wanted to make sure. She pulled her laptop over, opened it up, and searched for "how to reseal a jar of jam."

She found a few sites with varying instructions, but she was drawn to a forum on a jam maker's page where people discussed this very topic. People were asking about resealing a jar after you'd opened it but didn't want to finish the jam, or to add more sugar. No one was asking for instructions on how to reseal the jar if you'd added poison to the mix, but she assumed the process was the same in any case.

Okay, so if she had this right, Bridget would have needed to put the poison into the jars and then close them again and put them into a hot water bath to reprocess them.

That seemed straightforward enough... But wait. Cheryl's eye caught on something. One of the participants in this discussion, who seemed to be asking a lot of questions, was a user named SweetBlossom. She'd seen that name before. It took her a moment to remember where... And then it hit her. It was Bridget's user name for her Etsy shop. It was Bridget who was asking these questions about how to open and reseal a jar of jam. She looked at the date of the post. Her heartbeat sped up as she realized Bridget had been asking about how to reseal jars just two days before she'd swiped the jam from Naomi's shelves!

This was it. This was the proof she needed. This was the evidence that would crack open the police chief's open-and-shut case. He still hadn't called her back. Well, she would try calling the station one more time. It was nearly seven o'clock, so chances were the police chief was already home and eating his dinner. Meanwhile Naomi was still sitting in jail, and Cheryl wasn't about to rest until she got the real culprit behind bars. She'd call the station and talk to any officer who was on duty. If no one would talk to her, she would go down there herself and demand someone listen to what she had to say.

But when she called the station again, she was pleasantly surprised when Delores patched her through to Chief Twitchell. "He's just back at his desk," Delores said. "I'll put you through."

"What is it, Cheryl?" Chief Twitchell said, sighing. His voice was a bit raw, and she could hear his exhaustion.

"I know who put the poison in the jam," she said. "It's Bridget Marshall. I have proof, and . . . "

"Who is Bridget Marshall?" he said. He almost sounded like he was in physical pain.

"She's a rival jam maker. One of these hipster-city-girls-turned-country-princess things. She's been trying to get her jam on to people's shelves, and she finally got desperate enough that to eliminate the competition she put poison in Naomi's jam."

There was silence on the other end of the line.

"I have proof," she said.

Still, quiet.

"Why aren't you saying anything?" she asked.

"Because my mother taught me that if I don't have anything nice to say, to keep my peace."

"You don't believe me." The initial shock she felt turned quickly to indignation.

"Cheryl, I know you're upset about Naomi, but..."

"You said yourself you don't believe it's her, and now when I tell you I know who it is, you..."

"I never said I didn't believe it was Naomi," he said.

Cheryl felt like screaming. Maybe he hadn't in so many words, but he'd conveyed it.

"And do you hear what you're sayin'? A rival jam maker? Do you know how crazy that sounds?"

"What sounds crazy to me is keeping the wrong woman locked up when I'm telling you I know who the right one is. That must be one powerful state senator because the police chief I know would stand up for truth and justice, not be pushed around by some man who just wants to see someone—anyone—punished."

Again, there was silence on the other end of the line. Then he let out a long breath. "I'm sorry, Cheryl." He was quiet again for a moment. And then he spoke again. "I just came back from the scene of a grisly crash out on Route 39. A speeding car and a buggy. It was... It was not good. I'm still shaken by that, I think. It's hard to shift back to jam."

Cheryl forced herself to bite her tongue. It wasn't just jam they were dealing with here. It was intentional poisoning. Three people had ended up in the hospital because of this girl's actions, and they were lucky it hadn't been more. But Cheryl knew that he was exhausted and shaken by whatever it was he'd seen out at the accident site, and she knew getting derailed by arguing with his phrasing would only slow things down.

"I'm sorry about that. But please, you have to talk to Bridget."

"I can't do it tonight, Cheryl."

He didn't say anything more for a moment, but she'd heard a change in his tone. His voice had lost some of its edge, and she could hear the exhaustion again, coupled with something that sounded like remorse. But her triumph at getting him to listen to her was twinged with worry about the occupants of the buggy. She hoped it was not someone she knew, but in any case, she hoped the people would be okay. She knew cars speeding over the hills around here could sometimes come across slow-moving buggies they hadn't seen over a hill, and that could lead to devastating crashes. It was usually the Amish who were hurt in these cases. While the police chief was gathering his thoughts, Cheryl sent up a prayer for whoever had been involved in the accident. She prayed that God would bring healing and that whatever the injuries were, the victims would recover quickly.

"So," he finally said, "why do you think that this Bridget Marshall is behind the poison?" She heard him typing on the other end of the phone line.

"Here's what happened." Cheryl quickly explained how Bridget had gone to Naomi's basement; taken jars of jam and labels; unsealed the jars and added poison; reprocessed the jars;

made labels just like Naomi's and applied them to the freshly sealed jars; and then left jars of the tainted jam at the Swiss Miss, the Honey Bee, and Yoder's Corner in order to get Naomi's jam off the shelves to make room for her own.

She heard the chief sigh with frustration at more than one point in her story. And okay, she had to admit it sounded far-fetched. She'd thought so too, until she'd become convinced it was true.

"What's the proof?"

"Do you have your e-mail open? I'm sending you a link to a forum where they're discussing resealing jars of jam."

She sent him an e-mail, and she heard a little ding as it appeared in his inbox.

"Click on the link," Cheryl said.

"Okay..." He went quiet for a minute. "It's a bunch of women discussin' jam."

"Look at the date stamp on a post by SweetBlossom. The subject line is 'Will my jam jars reseal?'"

"Okay..."

"SweetBlossom is Bridget! That's the name of her Etsy shop. And she posted this question just two days before she stole the jam and the labels from Naomi. There's a very specific reason she was asking about resealing jars!"

The police chief let out a long breath.

"This is your proof, Cheryl? This SweetBlossom thing?"

"It's her! She's publicly posted about what she's planning to do!"

"Where does it say that she wants to reseal the jars after she puts poison in them? Where does it say, 'My name is Bridget Marshall of Tuscarawas County, Ohio, but you can call me SweetBlossom?'"

"It doesn't say those things specifically." Cheryl could feel herself getting frustrated again. "But it's her. You can prove it."

He sighed again. "This isn't proof, Cheryl. And as much as I want to believe you, it's not just me that you need to convince here. People are invested in this case all the way up the line to the top of the state government. I need somethin' that will hold up in court against some very powerful forces who feel that they have found their culprit."

She wanted to argue but decided that wasn't going to help her at this point. As her Southern momma used to say, you catch more flies with honey than with vinegar. She always struggled with that personally, but she saw the wisdom of it.

"What would be proof that would convince you then?"

He blew out a breath. "A confession. I think a confession from this other jam maker would be about what it would take to make them believe you."

"A confession, huh?"

"Yes, I'm afraid so."

"All right then," Cheryl said. She felt determination rising up inside her. "I'll get you a confession."

She felt triumphant as she said it, but as soon as she hung up the phone, she felt despair wash over her.

How in the world was she going to get a confession?

Well, the first thing to do would be to spend some time praying about it, she decided, so she prayed for Bridget, that the Lord would soften her heart and make her receptive to telling the truth. She prayed for Naomi, that she would keep her spirits up as she sat in jail. She prayed for the whole family, and especially for Levi, that he would get out of whatever funk he'd fallen into. When she finally said amen, she opened her eyes and saw that snow was falling softly outside. It looked beautiful in the pale moonlight, and she sat still and watched it for a few minutes. She didn't really feel any better after her prayer, but feeling good wasn't really the point. After a nice long talk with God, she had a renewed belief that God was in control and would work all things out for the good of those who loved him.

Then she started to push herself up when a noise from her computer caught her attention. It was Skype. Aunt Mitzi was calling! Cheryl felt a surge of affection rush through her, and she eagerly clicked to answer the video call.

"Aunt Mitzi!" Cheryl said as her aunt's face, tanned and happy, appeared on her screen. "How are you?"

"How's my favorite niece?" Aunt Mitzi asked.

Cheryl laughed. "The niece who currently has possession of your house and business is doing well."

"Like I said, my favorite niece." Mitzi laughed, a jolly, heartfelt laugh. "How's it going there?"

Aunt Mitzi was sitting in a room painted a bright shade of blue, and behind her Cheryl could see lush green plants growing outside the window. Cheryl thought about where to start, but suddenly trying to explain what was going on with Naomi or with Levi just seemed too hard. Instead, she said, "It just started to snow."

"*Oooh!* Let me see! Let me see!"

Cheryl smiled and picked up the laptop and moved it over to the window and turned it so the camera in the screen was pointed outside toward the streetlight.

"Oh my goodness," Aunt Mitzi said, sighing. "It's so beautiful, isn't it?"

And Cheryl agreed there was something ethereal, almost spiritual, about fluffy white snow as it fell.

"I miss it," Mitzi said.

"I know," Cheryl said. "I tried to figure out how to send you some."

"You did?"

Cheryl quickly explained how she'd looked into shipping her snow and ways for Mitzi to make her own snow.

"Well, none of that sounds very feasible, but I can't tell you how much I appreciate that you spent all that time thinking about me."

"Of course," Cheryl said, turning the computer away from the window to look at her aunt. "I wish I could have figured out a way to make it happen for you."

"You are so sweet to think of me." Her aunt brushed a piece of hair back from her face. "Now. Tell me about life there. How are you? How's the Swiss Miss? How's Naomi?"

Cheryl realized that her aunt didn't know anything about what had been happening with Naomi, so she filled her in on the jam, her search for answers, and Naomi's time in jail.

"Oh dear," Aunt Mitzi said. "Poor Naomi. I will be praying for her. And for her whole family." A breeze blew outside the window behind her, and a wind chime tinkled softly. "I don't know what's wrong with Sam. He should know better. Why, when I get back there, I'm going to give him a piece of my mind."

Cheryl knew Sam was Chief Twitchell's first name, though she'd never have the guts to call him that. "I guess he's under a lot of pressure to have a suspect in custody."

"Pressure my foot. There is no way sweet Naomi did this, and he knows it." She shook her head. "You keep digging, Cheryl. You'll find the truth. I believe in you."

"Thank you, Aunt Mitzi." She knew that Aunt Mitzi always believed in her, but hearing the words still made tears well up in her eyes.

"Now, that's not all that's bothering you."

Goodness. Her aunt was half a world away, and she could see something else was upsetting her. Either her aunt was very perceptive or Cheryl was incredibly transparent.

"I've burdened you with enough for today."

"It's no burden. I *asked* what was going on with you, remember?"

Cheryl thought for a moment. Her aunt had enough to worry about. She didn't really even know what to say. How could she complain about how things were going with Levi when everything about her relationship with him was so nebulous anyway?

"You haven't mentioned Levi yet," Aunt Mitzi said knowingly.

Cheryl sighed. It was like her aunt saw through her, to the very core of her.

"Things have been fine." Cheryl tried to dodge the question.

"But…?"

"But he's been kind of weird recently."

"Weird how?"

Cheryl patted the couch, and Beau jumped up beside her.

"Well, he's had kind of a temper."

Aunt Mitzi laughed, and then she smiled and gestured for Cheryl to go on.

"Like, I brought my old skis over to teach him and Eli to cross-country ski…"

"Oh my. I wish I could have seen that."

"Eli was awesome. Levi? Not so much. But I didn't mind. It was fun spending time with him. But he got all weird and frustrated, and he got kind of mad about the whole thing. He said it's not for him."

"Well, it is pretty rare for an Amish man to do something frivolous like this."

"Frivolous?"

"In their culture, skiing is frivolous. You have to acknowledge that."

Cheryl reluctantly nodded.

"The Amish are not a frivolous people." Aunt Mitzi nodded. "And I suppose I can understand why he might get frustrated about being shown up by his younger brother, and in front of the woman he wants to impress."

Cheryl couldn't help feeling a bit of pleasure at those words. Levi wanted to impress her. But then, if that was his goal, he was a long way off.

"Yeah, but I don't care if he's good at skiing or not," Cheryl continued. I just wanted to have fun with him. But he got all mad, and then it wasn't fun for anyone, and now he's mad at me."

"What makes you say that?"

"The way he was acting. Sullen, quiet. He wouldn't meet my eye. And the way he talked, like what he was saying was final and he didn't want me to argue with him."

"Sounds like an Amish man to me."

"But that's not Levi."

Aunt Mitzi looked like she wanted to say something but was forcing herself to bite her tongue. "What else?"

"And then when Naomi was arrested, the whole way there, he just didn't say anything. I could tell he was upset, but he just wouldn't say anything. I still can't get him to talk to me about it."

"I'm sure you can understand why he'd be upset at a time like this."

"Of course I do. But he's shutting me out. If he's upset, he should talk to me about it, not get sullen and ignore me."

Aunt Mitzi didn't say anything for a moment. And then, slowly, she offered, "Did Lance often open up about his feelings?"

Cheryl cringed to hear her ex-fiancé's name. "No. But he wasn't exactly a sterling model for a man."

"But he was a man. In my experience, most men aren't especially open with their feelings."

Cheryl knew that, but it wasn't the point. The point was that Levi didn't trust her enough to . . .

"How much time have you spent around Amish men?"

"I don't know. A decent amount, I guess."

"In your experience, are they generally forthcoming with their feelings?"

"No." She knew what her aunt was getting at, but she wasn't going to end it there. "I get that in their culture, men don't really talk about their feelings. They're strong and stoic and all that. I get it. It's just, if this relationship, or whatever it is, is going to go anywhere, he needs to trust me enough to tell me what's going on. But he's being totally moody, and I've never seen him like this before, and I don't know what this means."

"What do you mean?"

"Like, does he even want to be in a relationship anymore? I don't know. He won't tell me."

"Has he indicated anything of the sort to you?"

"He hasn't said it, but he's not saying anything, so how would I know?" She patted Beau absently. "But it's like in the past few days, I've seen a side of him I've never seen before. And I don't know what to do about it."

Aunt Mitzi didn't say anything for a minute. She seemed to be trying to come up with how to say something kindly. Then slowly she said, "Do you want my honest opinion?"

"Yes." But even as she said it, she wasn't sure she meant it. What if Aunt Mitzi wanted to say that she and Levi simply weren't compatible? It's something she'd been wondering secretly, but did she want to hear it from her aunt?

"I think you're scared."

"Huh?" Well, that hadn't been what she'd expected to hear.

"You're madly in love with this Amish man, and you've been hurt before, so you're scared that something is going to go wrong."

Cheryl didn't know what to say to that since she knew that it was true.

"You say you've seen a side of him the past few days that you've never seen before. His temper and his moodiness. Well, you know what I think?"

"What?"

"Thank goodness he has a temper. He wouldn't be human if he didn't get mad sometimes. And given what's going on with his family, I think he can be forgiven for being a bit moody." She paused, and Cheryl could see the leaves blowing in the breeze outside her window. "And I think it's really good that you're seeing this side of him, actually. If you guys are serious about trying to imagine a life together, you need to see the real Levi, not the idealized Levi you have in your head. If you guys even have a prayer of making this work, you need to know each other's flaws and love each other anyway. And this seems to me to be a good first step."

Cheryl took a minute to think through what her aunt was saying. Could she be right? That Levi's moodiness was a good thing? Well, maybe not a good thing exactly, but something it was good for her to see now? She did kind of idealize Levi in her mind, she supposed. Maybe she hadn't let herself really think about him as a whole person with flaws.

"The two of you are going to have a difficult enough road ahead of you," Mitzi said. "Not an impossible one, certainly, but you face more obstacles than many other couples. Don't add unrealistic expectations to the mix. Love that man for who he is, flaws and all, just like he loves you flaws and all."

Cheryl didn't realize she'd started crying until she sniffed. "But Aunt Mitzi, I don't have any flaws." Cheryl tried to brighten the mood.

At that, her aunt threw back her head and laughed. "Oh boy. It seems like it's not just him you need to open your eyes about."

Cheryl laughed. Okay, if she was honest, there might be one or two things she could work on personally.

"Thank you for talking with me," Cheryl said. "I really appreciate it."

"No, thank you for talking with me. It does my heart good." She glanced away from the camera on her computer as if checking the time. "Well, I should probably let you get to bed. It's getting late there."

"Yeah, I probably should go," Cheryl said. "But thank you again."

"You keep me posted on how things are going. Not just with Naomi, but with Levi too."

"I will."

"And if you figure out a way to send me some of that snow, you know where I am."

"I do. Thanks, Aunt Mitzi."

Cheryl ended the call and sat on the couch for a while, looking at the falling snow, thinking about what her aunt had said. Her insides felt like one of those snow globes. She'd been settled, but then someone had turned her upside down and scattered her thoughts every which way. As she waited for her emotions to settle back down, she had a thought. She turned it around in her mind and decided it might work, but she'd think more about it later. For now, she thought through what Aunt Mitzi had said.

Maybe she hadn't been seeing Levi for who he really was. Maybe she needed to let go of the ideal she had of him and accept and love him for who he really was.

Cheryl didn't know how to do that.

But she also knew that if there was any hope of a future for them, she needed to try.

CHAPTER TWENTY-ONE

Cheryl woke up early on Saturday morning, and she spent the morning making plans. Chief Twitchell had said he'd need a confession out of Bridget to get Naomi out of jail, so that was exactly what Cheryl was going to get.

Then when all of her preparations were finished, she got ready for work and went into the shop. She opened up the shop, and as soon as Lydia came in, Cheryl headed out. She prayed as she made the drive over to Bridget's house, asking God to bless her interactions and to give her the words to say to help her get the confession she needed. Cheryl knew she would only get one shot; if she couldn't get Bridget to admit what she'd done, who knew how long Naomi would stay in jail?

Cheryl drove carefully down the rutted dirt road, which was covered in a fresh layer of snow. She wasn't sure if these back roads ever saw a plow, and she was glad for the good snow tires on her car. Eventually, she pulled up in front of the house. There was no car in the driveway, but smoke rose out of the little black chimney that vented from the pellet stove. Hopefully Bridget was home—and home alone.

Cheryl grabbed her purse and the tote bag she'd packed this morning. She turned on her phone's voice recording app, slipped it into her coat pocket, and then she went up the porch steps and knocked on the door.

A few minutes later, the door opened. Bridget stood there, wearing jeans and several layers of sweaters, her eyes wide. "Hi, Cheryl."

"Hi, Bridget. I hope you don't mind me stopping by like this. I tasted some of the delicious jam you made yesterday, and I wondered if I could ask you some questions about it."

"Okay." She seemed uncertain. "Sure."

"I really loved the cranberry and sage flavor," Cheryl said, smiling like a maniac, trying to get Bridget to trust her enough to let her inside. Bridget seemed wary. With good reason, Cheryl thought. If she were Bridget, she'd be nervous too. But then again, Cheryl now stocked Bridget's jam in her store, so Bridget couldn't just lock her out.

"Come in," the girl said. "I'm just working on a scarf for my Web site."

Cheryl saw that the television was on in the living room, tuned to some news program, and a scarf of thick blue wool was lying on the battered couch. Bridget turned the television off.

"I brought some muffins," Cheryl said, holding up her tote bag. "Apple cinnamon. I made them myself this morning, so they're fresh."

"Oh, wow." The girl brightened at that. "Thank you."

Cheryl wondered again if Bridget got enough to eat. She looked so thrilled at the prospect of muffins that Cheryl wasn't sure she did. She led Cheryl to the table and indicated for her to sit down. "I'll make some tea. Peppermint again?"

"That sounds lovely." Cheryl sat down, and Bridget placed two plates on the table and then went to the sink to fill the kettle. While she was busy, Cheryl started unpacking the muffins she'd made and pulled out a jar of Naomi's strawberry jam. She'd wrapped it in newspaper to protect it, and she unpacked it now and set it on the table as well.

When Bridget had set the kettle on to boil and grabbed a couple of cloth napkins and a butter knife, she sat down across from Cheryl. When she saw the jar of jam, she blanched. Cheryl pretended she hadn't noticed.

"Your jam comes in such interesting flavors. How do you come up with the combinations?" Cheryl asked. She set a muffin on a plate Bridget had provided.

"Oh, well, some of it is what kind of fruit I can get," Bridget said. "At this time of year, it's mostly citrus, so I go with that. A lot of the jars I gave you I made over the summer, when peaches and strawberries were in season and priced reasonably."

"But how do you know what herbs and spices will go with the fruit?"

Bridget smiled, but it didn't reach her eyes. She was looking at the newspaper Cheryl had casually left on the table. It was the Thursday issue, in which the main headline had been Amish Woman Denies She Poisoned Jam; Four Still Hospitalized.

"I just go with what sounds good to me," she said. She was trying to appear unaffected, it was clear. But her eyes kept darting to the newspaper and the jar of jam, and Cheryl could see that she was nervous.

"My husband is always coming up with crazy combinations. Like he suggested wheatgrass and honey, but I stick with what sounds good to me."

Wheatgrass? What in the world was wheatgrass?

"Well, you do a good job," Cheryl said. She reached for one of the muffins and set it on her plate. "That's part of the reason I wanted to talk to you. I have some questions about making jam, and with my friend Naomi in jail right now, I don't know who else to ask." Never mind that she could have asked—in fact *had* asked—Naomi's daughters or basically any Amish woman she knew. She tried to affect a casual tone, like she'd just thought of something. "Did you hear about that? I think I mentioned it the other day. There was some jam laced with rat poison sold in a few places in town, and people ate it and got very sick. It was just awful."

"Yes, I remember. How terrible." She didn't look at Cheryl as she took a muffin from the center of the table and put it on her plate. "You said it was your friend Naomi's jam?"

Cheryl nodded. "It's been just awful. Rat poison, can you imagine? I had no idea rat poison was so bad. Actually, I had no idea people even *used* rat poison anymore. I grew up in the suburbs. We didn't use stuff like that." Cheryl laughed, trying to sound like this was all coming to her now, when in fact it was a script she'd carefully worked out in advance. "Do you know what rat poison does to a person?"

Bridget shook her head. "I'm from the suburbs too."

"It eats up your stomach and makes you bleed to death," Cheryl said. It was mostly true, and it sounded quite dramatic, she thought. "Even just a little bit can kill you."

"Oh." Had the girl turned a shade paler? It was hard to tell. "Wow."

"Thankfully, they were able to treat all of the people who had eaten some, and they seem to be recovering. But it's hard to know if there are more jars out there that we aren't aware of. That's why I had room on my store shelves for your jam because we took it all down just to be sure." She peeled the wrapper off one of the muffins and broke it open. "But anyway, since it was her jam, they've arrested my friend Naomi, and I am positive she didn't add rat poison to her jam."

With that, Cheryl reached for the jar of jam she'd brought and unscrewed the cap. She set it down, careful to place it just so, so the label faced Bridget. She saw Bridget studying the label carefully. As well she should.

Cheryl had gone over to the shop this morning and carefully studied the jars of jam she'd taken off the shelves and found a label that had been done in Bridget's hand. It had been difficult at first to notice the slight changes in the handwriting—Bridget's practiced hand was very good at mimicking Naomi's style—but once she knew to look for the loops of the y and the t, it wasn't so hard to find one that Bridget had done. Cheryl had very carefully steamed the label off one of the jars Bridget had laced with poison so that Bridget would see one of the labels she herself had made, and used superglue to affix it to a jar Cheryl had in her own pantry—one she was sure was untainted. Cheryl had taken a jar that was perfectly fine and dressed it up to look, if Cheryl's hunch was right, like one of the jars Bridget had tainted.

"I have an idea about what might have happened to the jam, and I wanted to run it by you." Cheryl picked up the knife and dipped it into the jam.

"Isn't that some of your friend's jam right there?" Bridget said. Her voice was a pitch higher than normal. "Are you sure that's okay to eat?" She tried to set her face into a relaxed pose, but the tension still shone through.

"Oh, this? Nah, this one is okay," Cheryl said. She broke her muffin into two pieces. "It's from my store."

To someone who didn't know better, that might seem like a perfectly reasonable explanation, but to someone who knew that poisoned jam had been on Cheryl's store shelves, it would be cause for concern. And Bridget sure looked concerned.

Cheryl proceeded to scoop out some jam with the knife and slather it on the muffin. Bridget looked like she was about to say something, and for a moment, Cheryl held her breath, but just then the teakettle whistled, and she popped up to shut it off.

"So what was it you wanted to ask me?" Bridget asked, pouring the hot water into two mugs.

Cheryl slathered jam on the other half of the muffin.

"Here's my idea," Cheryl said as she set her knife down. "I don't think the poison was put into the jam before she sealed the jars. My idea is that someone opened the sealed jars, added poison, and then resealed them and distributed them around town. But I don't know much about canning and making jam…again, from the suburbs"—Cheryl laughed—"and I wanted to know if that's possible. What do you think?"

"What do I think?" Bridget repeated. She picked up both mugs and carried them to the table, but her eyes were on Cheryl's muffin.

"Yeah. Is it possible that someone could have opened the jars after Naomi was done with them, added the rat poison, and resealed them?"

"I...suppose." She set the mugs down.

"Here, have some," Cheryl said, pushing the jam toward Bridget.

"You know, I have plenty of jam here," Bridget said. "Why don't I get some of that, and we can have that instead?"

"Oh, don't be silly. You need to sell that jam, not eat it," Cheryl said. "Besides, I already have Naomi's jam all over my muffin. There's no reason to waste some of your delicious jam when this is good enough for me."

With that, Cheryl picked up her muffin.

Bridget looked at the muffin, then down at the jar label again. She seemed to be trying to decide what to do.

Cheryl started to move the muffin toward her mouth.

Bridget seemed stuck, unsure.

Cheryl was about to take a bite. Bridget's eyes followed the movement.

Just at the last moment, Bridget said, "Stop!"

Cheryl stopped, put her hand down, and looked at Bridget, her eyes wide. "What is it?"

"I really think you should have some of my jam," Bridget said. Her voice was overly bright. "I have a great flavor I'm anxious for you to try. Blueberry port."

"Oh, wow, that does sound good," Cheryl said, nodding. "Well, we've got plenty of muffins. If you want to open that one too, I'd be happy to try it." And with that, Cheryl lifted up the muffin slathered with Naomi's jam and took a big bite.

Bridget froze. Cheryl continued chewing, but as she ate the muffin, she screwed up her face a little. She swallowed, took another bite, and made the same face. When she swallowed, she said, "Huh. For some reason this jam tastes a bit off. Can we try your blueberry port after all?"

Bridget was still frozen in place, but then something seemed to change.

"You have to get to the hospital," she said.

"Why?" Cheryl looked down at her muffin and shrugged and then took another bite.

"Stop *eating* that," Bridget said, her voice warbling. "You need to get to the hospital. It will take too long to call an ambulance. Here, give me your keys. I'll drive you." She popped up and moved toward the door.

"What are you talking about?" Cheryl said, staying seated.

"You just ate some of that jam. The stuff with the poison in it."

"What?" Cheryl knew acting wasn't her talent, but she tried to keep her voice natural. "What do you mean?"

Bridget's eyes welled up, and she looked like she was in physical pain. She looked at Cheryl again, took a deep breath, and then said, "I put the poison in the jam. It was stupid, I know. I didn't realize how bad it was. But that's one of the jars I put the poison in."

Cheryl felt like throwing up her hands and shrieking. She'd done it. She'd gotten the confession she needed. Naomi could go free. She hoped her phone had captured the confession, but in any case, she thought it was unlikely Bridget would recant her story now, judging by the tears streaming down her face.

"What do you mean?" Cheryl forced herself to continue to play innocent. "One of the jars... *you* put poison in?"

"I did it, okay?" She gestured for Cheryl to get up. "It was so stupid. I can't believe how dumb I was. I thought it would just make people a little sick, like food poisoning. I had no idea it could kill you." She gestured again for Cheryl to get up and come with her. "And you just ate some, so we have to get you to the hospital right away!"

"I..." Cheryl shook her head, continuing to feign confusion. "I don't understand. How can you tell this is one of the jars with poison in it?"

"The label," Bridget said impatiently. "I can tell because I had to redo the labels. I'll explain on the way to the hospital."

Cheryl was kind of touched at how insistent the girl was that they go to the hospital right away. She really did seem to want to keep Cheryl from getting sick, which made it easy to believe that she hadn't really meant to hurt anyone. But Cheryl still needed to get her to admit why she had done it.

Cheryl started to push herself up. "But..." She pursed her lips as she stood. "But why? Why in the world would you do something like that?"

"Because I was desperate," Bridget said. She moved around the table to grab Cheryl's arm. "I spent all this money making my jam, and then no one wanted to buy it. And we needed the money really badly. Carter was saying I needed to find a way to contribute more or we weren't going to be able to keep the electricity on, and I just thought..." She shook her head again. "Look, obviously I didn't really think. But my idea was that if Naomi's jam was off the market, people would take a chance on mine."

Cheryl didn't say anything, but she allowed Bridget to drag her toward the door. She needed to figure out how to end this before Bridget really did drag her to the hospital.

"I feel awful about it, especially since Naomi was so nice to me. And now she's sitting in jail. I just...I don't..." She pulled her purse off a hook by the door. "Where are your keys? I'm sorry, Cheryl..."

"It's okay," Cheryl said, stopping as they reached the door.

"No, it's really not. You need a doctor. We have to..."

"Bridget, it's all right."

"Oh, you know, maybe we should call an ambulance anyway since I've never driven your car and these roads are terrible. That might be quicker after all." She let go of Cheryl and pulled her phone out of her purse.

"Bridget. That jam I ate isn't poisoned."

Bridget was so busy with her phone that she didn't seem to hear Cheryl. Cheryl reached over and pulled the phone from her hands. "Bridget!"

The girl looked up, reaching for her phone.

"I put one of your labels on a jar that wasn't poisoned. I am going to be fine."

"What?" The girl's voice came out as a high, squeaky whisper. She processed what Cheryl had said.

"So...you knew?"

"I had a pretty good idea," Cheryl said. "But I wanted to be sure."

Cheryl watched as Bridget processed this. She couldn't even imagine what was going through her mind right now. Was she imagining the consequences of admitting what she'd done? Thinking about all she'd be giving up because she'd confessed?

Cheryl gave her time to work through it, and then, gently, she said, "Would you like to tell the police, or should I?" Cheryl wasn't sure what kind of reaction Bridget would have, but she braced herself in case it was violent.

Instead, Bridget stood still for a moment, and then fresh tears welled up. "I need to call Carter," she said.

Cheryl panicked. She didn't want to give Bridget's husband a chance to convince her not to go forward with the truth.

"You probably do need to call him. But let's do it from the car."

"I just..." She put a thin arm against the wall to brace herself. "I need to think for a minute."

Cheryl could understand that she felt overwhelmed. That she saw her whole world collapsing right in front of her. Cheryl hurt for her.

But then she thought about Kathy Kimble, still recovering from her hospital stay. She thought about the tourist who had fallen sick from the jam and the vitriol her husband had spewed at Cheryl. She thought about poor, sweet Naomi, whose name had been slandered, jam business decimated, who sat in jail right now for the crime Bridget had just confessed to. Cheryl needed to get Bridget to the police before anything happened to change her mind.

"My phone has been recording this whole conversation," Cheryl said as gently as she could. "So the police are going to find out either way. The question is whether you go in and tell them yourself, in which case they will probably have some leniency, or whether I call Chief Twitchell to come out here to pick you up. He won't be as thrilled about that."

Bridget nodded. She seemed to understand the stakes. But still she hesitated, looking around the small home.

Suddenly Cheryl felt a pang of sympathy. Everything this girl knew was about to change. She may or may not end up serving jail time—though it seemed likely, if the state senator had his way—but in any case, she would have a criminal record. She would likely have to spend everything she had on a good lawyer, and she didn't have much. Her marriage, like her husband, was young. Cheryl didn't know anything about Carter, but she did know that something like this would try any relationship. Bridget was scared. And rightly so.

"Would you like me to pray with you?" Cheryl asked.

At first Bridget didn't seem to hear. She was frozen, holding herself up with her thin arm. Then, all of sudden, tears spilled over and ran down her cheeks, and she nodded.

Cheryl moved closer to the girl and put her hands on Bridget's shoulders. Taking a deep breath, Cheryl prayed. She prayed for peace for Bridget, for understanding for Carter, for leniency from the law, and that, no matter what happened, God would be glorified.

Then, slowly, Bridget looked up. She pulled a small pack of tissues from her pocket and unfolded one, and then she swiped at her eyes. Cheryl watched as she then pulled out a small quilted bag and took out a tube of lip gloss. She smoothed it over her lips and then put the gloss and the bag back in her purse.

"Okay," she said, nodding. "I'm ready."

Cheryl had to laugh. But mostly she was grateful this whole situation was coming to a close. Naomi would be freed, no charges would be filed against the Swiss Miss, and once they made sure they had gotten rid of all of the tainted jam, Naomi's jam could be sold again.

The Lord worked in some interesting ways, she thought. She couldn't say she was thankful that this had all happened. They would all be dealing with the consequences of Bridget's poor decision for a long time to come.

But she also knew that when God was involved, grace and forgiveness abounded.

Yes, the Lord worked in mysterious ways.

And she was grateful He had worked here today.

CHAPTER TWENTY-TWO

By the time Cheryl was ready to close up the Swiss Miss for the day, Naomi was home, cleared of all charges. Cheryl had actually jumped up and down when Elizabeth called to tell her the news. Esther, who'd been ringing up a customer, let out a very un-Amish whoop. Rather than explain details to the confused customers in the shop, Cheryl simply said they'd had some good news, and they seemed to accept that.

Cheryl had driven Bridget to the police station that morning, where she'd confessed to putting rat poison in Naomi's strawberry jam. Chief Twitchell had avoided Cheryl's eye when she'd brought Bridget in, but as she got ready to leave, he quietly said, "Thank you." Cheryl knew it was the only acknowledgement that she'd been right she was likely to get, but it was enough. He'd promised to call New Philadelphia and see how quickly he could get Naomi freed.

And now she was home. Cheryl thought that her friend would want a quiet evening at home with her family, but Elizabeth had said that Naomi wanted Cheryl to come see her so she could thank her. Cheryl had offered to give Esther a ride home and promised to be there after they closed for the day.

Now after they'd closed down the register and swept the floors, Esther stood by the door, anxious to get home and see her mother.

But before they headed out, Cheryl did one more thing. She went over to the shelf that held the hand-carved toys, and she looked over each of the cleverly crafted snow globes. She examined the one that represented an Amish farm, holding it up to the light. It was still so hard to imagine that someone had carved each of these pieces by hand. The scene was gorgeous, peaceful, serene.

But it wasn't quite right. Cheryl set that one back down on the shelf and picked up the one that depicted the little town of Sugarcreek. There was the giant cuckoo clock and the sign that welcomed visitors to town. There were the shops along Main Street, and right at the center was the Swiss Miss, complete with its gingerbread trim and heart-shaped window. An Amish buggy was even parked right in front. She flipped it upside down, and tiny flakes of snow fell gently over the miniature version of the town.

This was it.

Cheryl took the snow globe to the counter and wrapped it into several layers of tissue paper. She'd send it to Aunt Mitzi on Monday.

It may not be the same as enjoying actual snow, but at least her aunt would be reminded of what it was like to watch snow falling on the little town she still considered home. Cheryl hoped that seeing it would also remind her of all the people here who loved her and were praying for her.

Cheryl tucked the snow globe into her purse, and then she and Esther locked up the shop and headed to her car.

Esther was chatty on the way out to the farm, and Cheryl listened as she explained the various games they played at Singings.

In some ways, it didn't really sound all that different from a typical high school party to Cheryl, except for the buggies and the long dresses.

Mostly, Cheryl was glad to see that the tension Esther had been carrying the past few days was gone. It was a relief to all of them that Naomi had been proven innocent. And Cheryl was grateful for the chatter, as it distracted her from the growing sense of dread she felt. She hadn't seen Levi since the scene in the barn the other day. She knew she would see him at the farm. Was he still upset? Was she? She didn't know what she would do when she saw him, but the knot in her stomach grew tighter the closer they got to the farm.

When Cheryl followed Esther inside the house, Naomi, typically stoic and reserved, wrapped her in a big hug. Cheryl was surprised but pleased.

"I cannot thank you enough, Cheryl," she said, pulling back. "Thank you for getting me out of there and for proving that I did nothing wrong."

"Of course. We all knew that you were innocent," Cheryl said.

"But you found the real culprit." Naomi pulled her into the kitchen and gestured for Cheryl to sit down at the kitchen table. Cheryl was glad to see that the men were all still out in the barn, and it was just Elizabeth and Esther and Naomi here in the kitchen. "And not only did you find her, you got her to confess. I cannot thank you enough."

"I cannot believe it was Bridget after all," Elizabeth said from the stove. She had just dumped a handful of noodles into a pot of boiling water and was stirring it with a wooden spoon. "It is shameful that she came in here and acted like she was our friend and meanwhile she was stealing Maam's jam and setting her up for a crime."

"She is young," Naomi said. "We all make silly mistakes when we are young."

Cheryl was impressed, as she so often was, at how gracious her friend could be. Here she was, just hours after being released from jail, making excuses for the girl who had betrayed her trust and set her up.

"She may be young, but that does not excuse her foolishness," Esther said. She had taken off her kapp, and her long dark hair spilled out over her shoulders.

"It does seem like she really didn't realize how dangerous rat poison is," Cheryl admitted. After hearing Bridget's tearful confession to the police, Cheryl had come to believe that she truthfully hadn't understood that she could have killed someone. Still, while she might not be a sociopath or something of that nature, she was most certainly immature.

"Did she not understand why there is a skull and crossbones on the package?" Esther asked. "Or what poison is?"

"She said she thought it was like food poisoning, where you get a little sick but then recover quickly." Cheryl shrugged. "Look. I'm not defending her. All I'm saying is that she didn't set out to land anyone in the hospital."

"Or the jail," Naomi added.

"I think she is still *dumm*," Esther said. Cheryl knew she meant Bridget was foolish.

"Esther," Naomi said, shaking her head. "When you speak, always remember that God is one of your listeners."

Esther nodded, chastened.

"I am just glad to be home. And I am very much looking forward to a good home-cooked meal. The food in that jail is terrible." She turned to Cheryl. "You will stay for dinner, *ain't so?*"

Cheryl had a lot of questions she wanted to ask Naomi about what her experience had been like. Had it been like the TV shows? What were the other prisoners like? Had she been locked up in her own cell? But she knew better than to ask those questions now, with her children around. Instead, she considered the invitation to dinner. Even if she wasn't sure where things stood with Levi, eating a delicious meal in this warm and snug home with the people she cared about sounded far better than curling up at home with Beau and a movie on Netflix.

"I would love to," Cheryl said. "Thank you."

They then asked Cheryl to recount how she'd gotten Bridget to confess, and she told the Miller women the whole story, from steaming off the label of one of the tainted jars to slathering the good jam on her muffin, trying to make Bridget believe it was a jar she'd poisoned.

As she was explaining how Bridget had tried to drag her to the hospital, the back door slid open, and Seth walked in, followed by Eli and Levi. Cheryl held her breath as Levi stepped in and saw her, and he gave her a tight smile. She wasn't sure how to interpret that, but at least it hadn't been a look of disgust or frustration, she thought, trying to console herself.

"Hello, Cheryl," Eli said, excitement on his face. "I have been practicing. I am getting quite good at skiing."

"That's what I've heard," Cheryl said, nodding. "I think there are some cross-country trails not too far from here that you should try out."

Seth had gone to the sink to wash his hands, and Levi was looking inside the refrigerator, but Cheryl could tell by his posture that he was listening.

"I would like to," Eli said. "But what I really want to try is going down an actual mountain. Take the ski lift up and ski down. There has got to be someplace like that nearby, right?"

Cheryl was pretty sure that the nearest place to ski downhill was several hours away, and she doubted Seth would allow him to go even if it were closer. But she didn't want to crush his dreams, so she simply nodded.

Seth said something stern to Eli in Pennsylvania Dutch, and it set Esther laughing. Cheryl looked to Naomi for an explanation.

"My husband does not believe this would be the best use of Eli's time or money," Naomi said, stifling a laugh. "And I have to agree with him." She leveled a look at Eli, one that was familiar to anyone who'd ever had a mother.

Cheryl was pretty sure that Eli would enjoy downhill skiing and be quite good at it, but she was also certain he had no idea how expensive it could be when you factored in the hotel and lift ticket. It seemed unlikely that Eli would get to experience the rush of wind on his cheeks as he zoomed down the mountain anytime soon, but you never knew.

"We will see," Eli said, and then he winked at Cheryl and walked through the kitchen toward the stairs.

"We will be eating shortly," Elizabeth called after her brother, and Eli nodded to acknowledge he heard her and headed up the stairs.

Esther had already stood and was walking toward the wooden hutch where the dishes were kept.

"Cheryl is staying for dinner," Esther said, looking at Levi knowingly.

"I am glad," Levi said. He shut the refrigerator door and turned to Cheryl. He gave her a smile, and she returned it. "Cheryl, would you be willing to show me how to do the snowplow now?"

Cheryl felt her shoulders relax, and tension she hadn't realized had been there flowed out of her body. She recognized that Levi was offering her an olive branch.

"That sounds perfect." She pushed herself up.

Levi waited for her and started toward the back door.

"Do not go too far. Dinner will be in just a few..."

Elizabeth was silenced by a swift kick from her sister. Elizabeth looked at Esther, wide-eyed, but Esther smiled at Levi and Cheryl innocently.

"Take your time," Naomi said. "Dinner will wait."

Cheryl went to the front to grab her coat and shoes, and a minute later she followed Levi out into the backyard. He had put his coat back on and held a kerosene lantern. The skis were leaned up against the back of the house. He led her over to them and handed her the lantern, and then he picked up both pairs of skis and boots and poles and carried them to the bench. They didn't speak, but the air between them was charged.

"The black skis really are better," Cheryl said. "Why don't you try that pair this time, and I'll put on the pink ones." A chill passed through her, and she wasn't sure if it was because of the cold air or the tension between them.

Levi nodded, and she helped get him fitted into the boots. Then she got her feet into the other pair of boots. She reached out to grasp the skis, but as she did, Levi spoke.

"I am sorry."

"What?" Cheryl looked to Levi. His face was so handsome in the warm glow of the kerosene lamp. He was looking at her, pressing his lips together.

"I should not have lost my temper. I have been acting badly all week, and I am sorry."

Cheryl took this in, and she nodded. Moonlight shone down on the layer of fluffy snow that covered the yard, and it sparkled all around them like thousands of tiny diamonds. The trees moved with a soft breeze, but the yard was quiet, save for the occasional noise from the barn.

"You were under an incredible amount of stress, and I should have realized that," Cheryl said. She adjusted her grip on the handle of the ski pole. "And I shouldn't have pushed you about skiing."

"It was not about skiing," Levi said. "I was frustrated about how difficult it was, and I was annoyed at Eli for finding it so easy. I was jealous. I got mad because of these things, not because of skiing." He shifted on the bench so he was angled toward her. "Actually, watching how much fun Eli has been having these past few days has made me think I would like to really learn. It may take more time and effort for me to get better at it than it did for Eli, but I want to try."

"Levi, I . . ."

"Please wait, Cheryl. Let me say this." He took a deep breath. "Last night Esther asked me what was wrong. She said I was acting strangely, and I told her about our conversation in the barn. She told me what I already knew, that I was wrong, and that I needed to apologize to you. I have now done that, but that is not enough. I need to explain what was really happening."

Cheryl wasn't sure what she was more surprised about, that he was apologizing or that he'd talked to his sister about his feelings. But she was delighted, in both cases.

"I was anxious about what was going on with Maam, and I was annoyed at how easily it seemed to come to Eli, but I was really upset because I wanted to do well for you. I wanted to be good at skiing because it is something you love. And I want to love the things you love."

He was sitting so close to her on the bench that she could feel the heat from his leg pressed against hers.

Cheryl held her breath, waiting to see if he would go on. Her thoughts were zooming around her mind. He wanted to love the things she loved. He wanted her to think he was good at something she enjoyed. He wanted to be with her.

"I am sorry I was short with you," he said. "I should not have let my frustration and worry about Maam affect how I acted toward you."

Just last night Cheryl had complained to Aunt Mitzi that it felt like she didn't know Levi. Now she was feeling that all over again, but for very different reasons.

Levi, like most Amish men, was typically quiet and stoic. He didn't talk about his feelings. He was strong and stable but not exactly expressive. But just because you don't usually show your feelings doesn't mean you don't have them. And it took a huge amount of strength to admit that you were wrong, Cheryl realized.

Which was why she needed to summon up her own strength now.

"I am sorry too, Levi." She could hear movement inside the house, and a splash of light spilled out through the window on to the snow, but they were far enough from the house that she was sure the family couldn't hear their conversation.

"What are you sorry for?" Levi asked.

"For expecting you to be something you're not," Cheryl said. "For expecting you to be perfect."

"You do not think I am perfect?" Levi gasped, but she could see laughter in his eyes.

"I like you even better now that I see you get angry sometimes too."

"Of course I do," Levi said. "I am human, you know."

"But I'd never seen it," Cheryl said. "And I love seeing different sides of you."

Levi didn't say anything for a moment. Then, slowly, carefully, he reached out and took her hand in his own. Cheryl's heart started beating faster, and she felt her cheeks flush. They both wore thick wool gloves, but she could still feel his body heat through them.

"If we are going to have any chance at a future together, we will need to know each other well and accept each other's faults," he said.

Cheryl nodded. She wanted to make a joke about how she didn't have any faults, but she couldn't get her mouth to form a coherent sentence. He was talking about a future together. He wanted a future with her, just like she wanted one with him.

It would take more than accepting one another's faults for a relationship between them to work. There were so many barriers to overcome, so many big, life-changing decisions to be made. But it would be worth it, she hoped. She had to believe so.

"Your biggest fault that I can see right now is that you don't know how to ski," Cheryl said, and Levi cracked a smile.

"I guess we had better fix that." Levi reached for the pair of black skis that sat next to the bench, and Cheryl helped him snap his boots into them. Cheryl then slipped her own skis on and then helped Levi to his feet.

"How do you feel?" she asked.

"Like I am about to make a huge fool out of myself." Levi said it so seriously that Cheryl had to laugh.

"You're going to do fine."

"I do not know about that. But I am glad to be here spending time with you anyway."

She was still holding on to his hand, and she didn't let it go. Moonlight spilled down all around them, and the whole world glimmered a beautiful, ethereal silvery white. The barn, silhouetted against the night sky, stood tall and proud. Beyond the yard, the farmland rolled out, acre after acre of smooth white snow.

Cheryl looked up at the man next to her, and her breath caught in her throat. He was so handsome in the moonlight. "I'm glad to be here with you too," she said and squeezed his hand gently. Sometimes she couldn't believe how lucky she was to have ended up here, in this wonderful community, with these incredible friends. With this incredible man.

No, right now, Cheryl couldn't think of any place she would rather be than right here in Sugarcreek.

AUTHOR LETTER

Dear Reader,

Journeying back to Sugarcreek in these books is such an escape for me. I so enjoy getting a chance to glimpse a world where life moves at a slower pace, where community and family come first, and where faith is a central part of life. I also love learning new things, like how to make jam. I have never made jam. I didn't think I even liked jam until a few years ago when I tried some apricot jam that made me realize I actually do like *good* jam—homemade jam, like Naomi would make. Writing this book gave me the perfect excuse to branch out and try strawberry jam—and I realized I liked it too. A whole new world has opened before me.

The part of this story that is based on my real life is Levi's trouble with skiing. I tried skiing once. My friends took me to the top of a mountain—no lessons, no advice, nothing—and told me to go for it. After some dramatic falls, I rode the rest of the way down on a rescue snowmobile. A few years ago, I even tried cross-country skiing, which seems more my style anyway, and ended up with a broken tailbone. So I certainly identified with Levi's struggle to figure out how to keep himself upright and his struggle to understand why anyone does this ridiculous sport in the first place. It's so much more pleasant to sit inside and drink cocoa, in my (totally unbiased) opinion.

I hope you enjoy this story as much as I enjoyed writing it!

Best,
Elizabeth Adams

ABOUT THE AUTHOR

Elizabeth Adams lives in New York City with her husband and two young daughters. When she's not writing, she spends time cleaning up after two devious cats and trying to find time to read mysteries.

Fun Fact about
the Amish or Sugarcreek, Ohio

When I first proposed the idea of a storyline about Levi and Eli learning to ski, I wasn't sure how feasible it would be. I thought it was fun to imagine Levi zooming down a hill, dark coat flying behind him, and Eli goofing off on a ski lift. After talking to a few people, I realized that while it wouldn't be forbidden for them to go skiing, most Amish would have little patience for the cost (gear, ski rental, lift ticket, resort costs) and effort (several hour drive to the mountain) involved in downhill skiing. So I decided to have them do cross-country skiing, which seemed a bit more plausible.

But I also discovered that the Amish do take vacations. Sarasota, Florida, is a popular Amish destination, and families will travel there to spend time relaxing in the sun. Most of the time, Amish vacations involve visiting far-flung friends and family. They don't often go to Disney World or fly to Hawaii to experience its renowned beaches, but they will travel to see relatives or friends who've moved away and stay in their homes. I love the idea that people—not attractions—are the main motivation for travel. It always seems that the more I learn about the Amish, the more I learn about how I wish my life could be.

SOMETHING DELICIOUS FROM OUR SUGARCREEK FRIENDS

Cheryl's Apple-Cinnamon Muffins

Muffins:

2 cups all-purpose flour

1½ teaspoons baking powder

¼ teaspoon salt

2 teaspoons ground cinnamon

½ cup (1 stick) unsalted
butter, room temperature

1 cup granulated sugar

2 large eggs

1 teaspoon pure vanilla extract

½ cup milk

2 cups peeled, cored, and
diced apples

Topping:

½ cup butter, melted

¼ cup granulated sugar

¼ cup ground cinnamon

Preheat the oven to 375 degrees. Grease or fill muffin cups with paper liners. In a small bowl, combine the flour, baking powder, salt, and cinnamon. In a separate bowl, use an electric mixer to cream the butter and the sugar until light and fluffy. Add the eggs one at a time, and then add the vanilla. Gently mix in the flour mixture, alternating with the milk. Try to stir as little as possible.

Gently stir in the apples. Drop the mixture into muffin tins. Bake about thirty minutes or until done.

Meanwhile, in a small bowl, melt the butter and cool it a bit. In a separate bowl, combine sugar and cinnamon. When the muffins are done, carefully take each muffin and dip it in the butter and then in the sugar and cinnamon and allow to cool.

Read on for a sneak peek of another exciting book
in the series Sugarcreek Amish Mysteries!

A Play on Words
by Emily Thomas

Cheryl Cooper buttoned up her coat as she made her way to the car. It was already mid-March, but it sure didn't feel like spring was coming anytime soon. The weatherman had called for a light dusting of snow to fall this evening, killing Cheryl's hopes that flowers would soon be blooming and the jackets would soon be retired. She should know by now that winter often lasted through April here in this part of Ohio, but that didn't stop her from wishing for warmer days. She'd raced home from church that morning and changed from her Sunday-best dress into flannel-lined jeans and a bulky sweater, but she still felt chilled to her bones.

Cheryl climbed into her car and cranked up the heat. Then she backed the car out of the driveway and paused at the end to admire the little cottage where she lived. It had finally begun to feel like home. She pulled out into the street and started driving toward town.

She loved the way the quaint village of Sugarcreek looked blanketed in snow, so maybe one last snowfall wouldn't be so bad. After all, Sugarcreek was also known as "the little Switzerland of

Ohio," and snow certainly went along with that. Cheryl mentally added hot chocolate to her long grocery list as she made her way down the sleepy street.

Sometimes she couldn't believe that Sugarcreek was really home now. A year and a half ago Aunt Mitzi had accepted the call to become a missionary in Papua New Guinea, and she'd offered Cheryl the chance to run her store, the Swiss Miss. Cheryl had been living in Columbus and hadn't been sure how long she'd want to stay in this small town, where the population was Amish, but somewhere along the way, Sugarcreek had started to feel like home.

Cheryl slowed down as she arrived at the grocery store. She passed the section of the parking lot reserved for horses and buggies and snagged a spot right in front. The novelty of living and working among the Amish had finally worn off some, and seeing the special parking area didn't jar her like it used to. Today she noticed the area because it was empty. The Amish would be with their families on the Lord's Day today, so not many would be out and about, and they certainly wouldn't be shopping on a Sunday unless it was a real emergency. Cheryl felt a bit guilty shopping today herself, thanks to the influence of her Amish friends, but her cupboards were truly bare.

Before she'd even turned off the car, her phone rang in her purse. She dug it out and glanced at the caller ID on the screen.

Lacey Landers.

It still gave Cheryl a tiny thrill that she had the phone number of a celebrity saved to her contacts. "Hello." Cheryl had met the movie star when Lacey had come to town to research a role for a movie set in Ohio's Amish country. They'd become quite friendly when the tour group she'd been traveling with had gone missing, and Lacey had helped Cheryl and her Amish friend Naomi search for the missing busload of people.

"You are *not* going to believe where I am right this minute." Lacey could always be counted on to get right to the point.

Cheryl laughed. "Let me guess. You're taking a spring break in some kind of tropical location?" Just last week, one of the celebrity news shows had shared photos of Lacey paddleboarding somewhere in the Caribbean.

"Not even close." Lacey let out a huge sigh. "I'm at a car rental place." She paused dramatically and inhaled. "In *Canton*."

Cheryl widened her eyes. "Canton, Ohio?" That sure wasn't tropical. Canton was only a little over a half-hour drive from Sugarcreek.

"I'm sorry I didn't tell you sooner. Everything just happened so fast." Lacey giggled. "You know how things go. One minute you're in Cabo and the next, Canton."

Yeah, that didn't sound familiar to Cheryl, but there was no point in trying to explain it to Lacey. Their versions of normal were very different. "Are you in the area to visit your grandparents?" Lacey's grandparents lived in an assisted living facility in nearby Dover.

"Kind of…" Lacey trailed off. "It's a long story. Any chance you'll be home in about an hour and a half? I'll explain in person."

"Sure. I'm getting a few groceries now, but I'll be home shortly."

"Perfect," Lacey said. "I'll see you soon."

Cheryl ended the call and hurried into the store. It had been several months since she'd heard from Lacey, other than a Christmas card. Aside from reading the occasional celebrity news story, she had no idea what Lacey had been up to, but she was willing to bet she was about to find out all the details. In very dramatic fashion. Lacey didn't do anything quietly. Cheryl had to smile at the thought. When Lacey had been in Sugarcreek awhile back, there'd never been a dull moment.

Just over an hour later, Cheryl was back home brewing a pot of coffee. When the doorbell rang, Cheryl wiped her hands on a yellow dish towel and hurried to the front door. She opened it to reveal a beaming Lacey.

The actress flung herself at Cheryl and gave her a big hug. "I'm *so* glad to see you."

"I'm glad to see you too. Now come on inside and tell me what you're doing in Canton. Might it have to do with a handsome FBI agent who lives in Ohio?"

Lacey's cheeks turned pink. "Not entirely."

Roy Neal, an FBI agent based out of Columbus, had worked on the case of the missing tour bus, and in the process, had fallen for Lacey. And vice versa.

Lacey gestured at a bag slung over her shoulder. "You're not allergic to dogs, right?"

"No." Cheryl ushered Lacey inside and closed the door. "Although Beau isn't their biggest fan."

At the sound of his name, her Siamese cat, Beau, peered around the corner. He stuck his nose up in the air and disappeared back into the kitchen.

Cheryl laughed. "I guess he isn't interested in a new friend."

Lacey unzipped one end of the dog carrier, and a little white face peeked out. "I couldn't leave Beckett at home this time."

Cheryl reached out and scratched behind the dog's left ear. "What kind is he?"

"A Yorkie mix. I rescued him a few months back, and now I take him with me whenever I can." She shrugged. "Since I'll be here for three weeks, I decided to bring him along. Thankfully my hotel is pet friendly."

"Three weeks?" Cheryl asked. "You're not researching another Amish role are you?" She poured them both a cup of coffee and they settled down on the couch. Beckett sniffed around and then settled at Lacey's feet.

Lacey shook her head. "Nope. But I will be getting back into my Amish character." She tucked a strand of glossy dark hair behind her ear. "Have you ever read the book *Simply Sugarcreek*?"

Cheryl thought for a moment. "I don't think so."

"It's about an Amish girl who finds out she was adopted and has a non-Amish family who wants to meet her. It's really well-written."

"It sounds fascinating."

"It is good. And now *Simply Sugarcreek* is headed to the Broadway stage. But first, it will debut right here in Sugarcreek." Lacey beamed. "And *I'm* the star."

"That's amazing! Congratulations." Cheryl remembered Lacey sharing her dream of starring on Broadway. Now, she was thrilled to know that her friend would be able to experience that dream come true. "Television star, movie star, recording artist, now stage actress." Cheryl grinned. "You're covering all the bases."

Lacey's list of television movie roles was pretty impressive. She'd portrayed everyone from a cop to a cupcake baker, but admittedly some of the movies hadn't been Oscar-worthy. "It's like no one realizes that I've grown up. I'm hoping this role on Broadway will change that."

Over the years, Lacey had definitely taken a beating from the tabloids. They scrutinized everything she did or didn't do. Cheryl had never thought about the downside of being a celebrity until she'd met Lacey.

"I'm sure taking on Broadway will finally silence some of those critics." Cheryl patted her arm. "But why is some big Broadway play premiering here?"

Lacey smiled. "Well, the story is set in Sugarcreek, after all. But, also, the director saw my last movie—the one where I played an Amish girl—and he thought I pulled it off quite well. It's kind of funny, because he normally directs movies for the big screen, but he's been dabbling in theater over the past few years. When he got the chance to direct this production, he really wanted me for the role. Like, he didn't want to take no for an answer." She grinned. "So I felt like I had some bargaining power. A lot of Broadway shows start off-Broadway. This is just a little more off-Broadway than normal."

"This certainly is off-Broadway. Where will it be performed?"

"It will be at the Amish Country Theater just outside of Sugarcreek. And it's great, because this way we'll work out all the kinks before it opens in New York." Lacey took a sip of her coffee. "I wanted it to start off here because my grandparents would never be able to travel to New York to see me, but I figure they can come to Sugarcreek for opening night." She smiled. "They are so excited. Nana is blazing through every online shopping site she can find in search of the perfect outfit."

Cheryl laughed. She'd met Walter and Clara Landers when Lacey had been in Sugarcreek the last time. They were so proud of their granddaughter. No doubt, being able to go to an opening night of one of her performances would be one of the highlights of their lives. "That is great."

"I sure hope so. Though I don't know, it seems like this production is cursed."

"What do you mean?"

"I'm joking, mostly," Lacey said. But Cheryl could see by the shadow that crossed her face that she wasn't entirely. "It's just that several things have already gone wrong, and we haven't even had the first rehearsal yet."

"Like what?"

"Like the funding for the show almost fell through, though I think it's safe for now, thank goodness. There was a big mix-up with the scripts, where each of the leads was sent a different version of the script, so we all memorized different versions of our lines. They realized it last week and sent new scripts out, but by then we'd already committed the old ones to memory, so it's hard to unlearn those. And the costume designer who was supposed to be responsible for all the costumes broke her collarbone and had to stay in New York."

"Oh dear."

"That's actually part of why I wanted to talk to you. I told Adam, the director, that your friend Naomi is an amazing seamstress. I thought she might be willing to help us get the costumes ready."

Cheryl mulled this over. Naomi Miller didn't know—or care—much about things like Broadway.

"Most of the costumes are Amish outfits anyway, and having someone Amish make them just makes sense. That way they're authentic."

But Naomi could sew. Boy, could she sew. She could make Amish clothing in her sleep.

"I could ask her," Cheryl said.

"Of course Adam would pay her well. She might need assistants to help, and the show could pay for that too. Maybe her daughters? Or some of her Amish friends? Whatever she needs. We just really need these costumes made. "

Cheryl thought Naomi would at least consider it, given those conditions. She may not care about Broadway, but she was a shrewd businesswoman, and she was always willing to help someone in need.

"I'll talk to her tomorrow and let you know what she says."

"Thank you, Cheryl. I knew we could count on you." Lacey clapped her hands together, and Cheryl noticed something.

"Lacey!" Cheryl gasped. There was a ring on her fourth finer. A gorgeous diamond ring. "What is that?"